VIRUSZ-19

HALIM ABOUTAJ

BRITAIN 2029:

We are a decade on from Brexit, the biggest political and economic disaster in British history. The U.K. has been plagued with constitutional and financial instability and the Parliamentary system has been dismantled entirely. Opposition towards the Government has been outlawed; the country is run by a fascist regime accused of genocide and war crimes. The monarchy has been removed; democracy is a distant dream. Brainwashed and indoctrinated by the propaganda regime of the Ministry of Information and Public Communications, the British Public remain unaware of the problems plighting their nation. The climate crisis has spiralled out of control, mass flooding events are common, killer heatwaves the norm and arctic – like winters are as certain as the sunrise. Tens of thousands die each year as antibiotics no longer work. Children sleep orphaned on the streets. A quarter of the country live in extreme poverty. The population has exploded in the last decade. The number of unemployed has hit the millions.

The country is on the brink of disaster.

THE MISSING
2024 - 2029

A cold wind blew through the empty streets. The only noise – the 'tink tink' of a cooling engine in the distance. A man sat, swathed in blankets, shivering under a flickering streetlight. He looked up as the sound of heavy boots slapping the cobbles pierced the silence.

A struggle. The men in the boots grabbed the man. The world slept as he was bundled into the back of a van, blindfolded and gagged.

The engine rumbles into life once more. And soon enough, it's as if no one was ever there at all.

Prologue

Jonathon Percival sat at his desk, his new position as CEO of BioFlex Medical and Military Solutions still sinking in. He flipped through some of the files on the table; projects that needed completing, people that wanted their 'problems' fixed, governments that wanted to destroy others. Several folders caught his eye – the "Hollowgram Project" – something he'd been working on for several years already, but his new authority gave him total control over the operation. And then "VIRUS Z-19" – his newest development yet. A new virus, a new threat, something that couldn't be stopped by even the strongest of antibiotics. A virus that not only infects and weakens the host, but allows them to live forever in a mindless, cannibalistic manner. Someone deep within the British Government approached him and asked him to design them a virus that could "solve a problem" – his job wasn't to ask questions, just to obey. They wanted a virus that at most could only infect one in every five and reanimate those who die from the sickness. Jonathon followed without question.

Initial tests of VIRUS Z-19 were looking promising for him – 6 weeks of continued isolation without food or water and the host was alive and rabid–like;

—

snarling, kicking and biting like a crazed animal.

Peering at the live CCTV feed on his computer screen, he gave the command to send another human test subject into the cell.

His eyes fixated on the screen; Jonathon watched as the new test subject was shredded by Patient Zero. Blood splattered everywhere and yet the shredded remains of the new test subject arose and fumbled round the room, snarling and foaming at the mouth.

Success.

Scraping his chair back on the cold metal floor, Jonathon walked towards the door, pulling on a coat and hat. Hurrying down the empty corridors of the BioFlex compound, excitement bubbled in his stomach as he drew closer to his laboratory. He reached the cell where Patient Zero was being held, but as he rounded the corner his excitement turned to unease.

Something was wrong. His eyes dropped to the floor and leading in the direction he'd just come from was a trail of blood, fresh wet blood.

He drew his eyes up to the cell containing the infected hosts. The door was wide open, still swaying slightly. Blood dripped from the twisted remnants, flesh hanging like bunting.

Reaching for his gun, Jonathon peered around the corner. The twisted, shredded bodies of his scientists lay twitching on the floor with blood spilling in every direction.

Their re-animated, mindless zombie state left them snarling and snapping at his heels, but they were too broken to attack. He unleashed a torrent of bullets and the grizzled scientists slumped motionless.

'So, they can be killed,' he thought.

But he had a much bigger problem on his hands. If Patient Zero and the others escaped, then they could start a pandemic that would cripple the world. It wasn't ready to be released yet. Grabbing another gun from one of the dead scientists, Jonathon ran out of the laboratory and back down the corridors. The trail of blood was getting stronger; fresh pools of blood were gathering around his feet. Gun cocked, he peered around the corner afraid of what monster may be lurking.

But the screams and shrieks of fear and anguish told him everything.

The escaped test subjects had attacked the BioFlex staff – dozens of them lay twitching and snarling on the floor, as the brutal virus took root in their bodies. Blood gushed in torrents and a heavy stench hung in the air.

All throughout the building the infected roamed, attacking and poisoning anyone they came into contact with.

Soon enough, there was barely a healthy living soul left in the building. Pops of gunfire echoed in the corridors but unless you knew where to shoot, no gun would stop those monsters from destroying you.

Shaking with terror, Jonathon ran back to his office shooting down anyone and anything that came into his path. He bolted the door shut and dragged all the furniture he could in front of the steel door. He'd be safe, for now. Loading up his computer, he sat back down and watched through the last few hours of CCTV footage from the lab. And then he saw it – the new kid thought that he'd open the cell containing Patient Zero. But why? Well, that remained to be seen.

The infected immediately sprung out, shredding the unsuspecting scientists in seconds, leaving their dying bodies twitching and shaking on the floor.

He slammed his fist on the table with anger, leaving a small dent. Reaching into his desk he pulled out a briefcase containing three vials... in case anything was ever to go wrong with the experiments. One for him, one for his wife and one for his baby daughter, Audrey. He stabbed the needle into his arm, draining the vaccine into his body.

He was protected from the virus, but not from the monsters that he had created.

His next task was to try and lock down the building – no one was getting in or out. With a great hiss, the giant steel doors slid into place and locked shut with a powerful electromagnet – so long as this building had power, the world would be safe from the horrors within. But deep down, he knew that this virus could never be contained. Something would happen, something would result in the catastrophic destruction of civilization.

It was later that night when that 'something' occurred. A violent storm raged outside, thunder boomed across the city as lightning flashed a brilliant white, illuminating the night sky.

Rain pelted against the windows and the wind howled through the corridors, blending with the groans and snarls of the infected. A shivering Jonathon sat on the sofa-bed, huddled against an electric heater for warmth.

All at once, the lights went out and the heater started to go cold. The building had no power.

Terrified, Jonathon watched out of his window as the

—

steel door that had barricaded the infected inside slumped open.

The creatures, drawn towards the blinding lights and deafening roars of the storm spilled outside, illuminated by the violent flashes of lightning. Jonathon could only look on in horror as his creations began to escape.

Where were the back-up generators? Why hadn't they come on yet? More and more of the undead staff of BioFlex spilled into the grounds – he had to do something. Kicking aside his makeshift barricade, he grabbed all the guns he could and stepped outside.

Several of his former colleagues dragged their bloody, rotten bodies towards him – without hesitation, Jonathon opened fire. Their corpses dropped to the floor as he ran for the exit, shooting indiscriminately at anyone in his path.

But most of them seemed to be outside already.

He fumbled in his pocket for a second, and then brandished a shiny metallic orb. He pulled the pin out of the grenade and tossed it into the crowd of undead employees. An explosion of body parts, blood and fire filled the darkness just as the backup generators roared into life. Nothing appeared to be moving out there. Jonathon made his way back to his office, exhausted.

He sat back down in his chair and pulled up the perimeter CCTV. Nothing seemed to be moving. Relief washed over him as he appeared to have it under control.

But as he buried his head in his hands, he failed to notice a zombified BioFlex worker pick himself up and drag himself away from the compound, into London. Sitting on his chair, he gazed upwards, quietly contemplating what to do next.

His thoughts were broken as the quiet chime of his phone filled the silence.

He had been expecting this call.

"Jonathon." A tense, cold voice emerged from the speaker.

He hunched forwards, tapping his fingers on the desk. "Listen, I can explain. Just give me a day, I'll clear this all up. Something happ-" His pleas were interrupted by the voice.

"No excuses this time, Jonathon. You have had enough chances. Now we have to clear up your mess."

"But all of my research is in here. If you destroy it, I'll lose it all. I WILL LOSE EVERYTHING."

"Get out now. The planes are on their way." Disinterested in his concerns, the room went silent as the voice hung up.

He stood up, dragging his gun across the desk as he made his way to the door. Gathering his most precious papers, he took one last look at his office before running for the exit.

Acutely aware of just how little time he had to get out, he sprinted down the endless corridors, his footsteps echoing across the walls.

He was panting, sweat pouring down his face, stars in front of his eyes.

The dull thud of his fall was lost in the frenzied snarl of the Infected surrounding him. He lay helpless as his papers swirled around him, stained with the blood of these grizzled creatures.

He had mere minutes left to make it out alive.

His gun lay to his left, just out of reach. Flailing uselessly in the pools of blood, his fingers brushed against the barrel. The Infected were ready to attack, pinning him down in every direction. A sigh of relief. His hands closed on the gun, pulling it back towards him. Lifting it above his head, he fired at the undead workers crouching over his body. One by one, their grip slackened as he managed to get to his feet.

He glanced back at the entirety of his life's work laying uselessly buried under piles of bodies and pools of blood.

As he reached the entrance, the piercing whine of a drone told him he had just seconds to run. Panting and wheezing, Jonathon flung himself through the door and onto the cold and wet tarmac as the building exploded in a hellish inferno behind him.

The blast echoed across London and the compound burned behind him.

In the distance the faint wail of fire engines rang out, but the most that they would assume is that there was a gas leak in one of the labs – no one apart from those in the shadiest branches of world governments knew the true nature of BioFlex and the pure evil that they have unleashed into the world.

company's headquarters that blew up on the outskirts of London.

Apparently, everyone inside the building died after a massive gas explosion destroyed the complex. Anyway, I had more important things to worry about – school starts in less than an hour and I hadn't even had breakfast yet!

I rushed downstairs, throwing my books in my bag and straightening my tie. Glancing in the mirror, I pulled my hair back and went to grab some breakfast – my mum was already sitting at the table, sipping at a glass of water.

"Morning Evie," slurred my mother, still clearly drunk from last night. "How're you doing? Looking forward to the first day back at school?"

I looked up from my plate to glare at her, as if to ask her if she was crazy. For the record I wasn't, in any way, looking forward to this morning.

The grey, colourless and monotonous humdrum of daily routine seemed a world away from the whimsical weeks of summer.

I tried the TV again, hoping that the power had come back so I could distract myself from my sorry excuse for a mother. It flickered into life, bringing up the State News channel.

Turning my attention to the headlines, the main story of the morning was the explosion at the medical company – Bioflex, I think they said.

Images of the burned, mangled bodies of the former employees filled the screen.

I could feel my breakfast rising back up my throat.

I quickly turned the TV off and opened the fridge to try to make my lunch for the day. The only thing left was a mouldy tomato, and I'd used the last of the bread for breakfast.

So, Mum hadn't been to the foodbank like she'd been promising. She's barely left the house since Dad vanished last year. Then the depression started, then the drinking and now only God knows what. Probably drugs.

I picked up my bag and stormed out of the house, just desperate to get away. She always acts as if she was the only one hurt by Dad's disappearance, but I still need her.

He went missing last year after he got made redundant... he managed to hang on to his job during the height of the Great Recession, but they decided that "it wasn't financially viable" to keep him anymore. Just another expendable component in their vast machine.

I looked down at the recycling bin – 3 more empty bottles had been added overnight. She never tells me how much she drinks, attempting to hide her habit, her addiction. I'm worried about her, she's not coping. And I've got no idea where she gets the alcohol from these days, it's so expensive in the shops and the foodbank only gives us half a bottle of wine at Christmas.

Trying to throw these thoughts from my mind, I meandered down the street until I reached my friend's house.

I've known Freddie since forever, we grew up together and we've always been there for each other.

"Hey!" called a voice. "Oi, I'm up here!" I looked up, and saw Freddie hanging out of the window. I smiled back, giving him a wave.

"Happy birthday!" I yelled up at him. He appeared at the window again, nodded and disappeared. Moments later, the door swung open and he was standing there, panting and ready to go.

"Sorry 'bout that," he wheezed. "Woke up late… alarm didn't go… power cut again"

"Yeah right," I laughed. "You're just lazy. You'd sleep all day if you could."

"Ah, you've got me there – I definitely would."

We made it to school just in time, the bell chiming as we burst through the door, earning us disproving glances from our new form tutor.
"God, she looks miserable," I whispered to Freddie.

The rest of the day seemed to melt into one long, boring blur, listening to lectures about how important your A – Level years are and that no opportunity should be wasted, et cetera, et cetera. The usual run of the mill start of term reminders and warnings.
Later that evening, I flopped onto the sofa and turned on the TV.
The State News Channel was still up from this morning, and tonight's headline was about how the UK was more financially, economically and socially better off approaching the tenth anniversary of Independence Day.
No one believed it; even the news anchor didn't look particularly convinced. But you could never challenge them. There were rumours, people were too scared to speak out.
Even just by thinking about it I feel uneasy, as if someone will arrest me just for a thought.
They then switched to a story about the European War,

about how Britain and her allies were winning on every corner of the Continent. Depressing.

The screen cut back to the studio, ready to deliver another bout of miserable reports.

"And now, the special report on the Charlie McIntosh and Dominic Carter summit. We take you live to Washington.'

The voice of Carter filled the room. "It has been my honour to spend the day talking to my good friend Charlie... very good, very informative – he's a good man. We are very pleased, very happy, to announce that our energy crisis will come to an end.

From tomorrow, British and American corporations will resume large scale coal mining

in various regions in both great countries – supporting American industries. WE ARE GOING BACK TO COAL!"

A protestor broke onto the stage, waving a banner and screaming at the camera.

"DON'T BELIEVE THEM! The world is already choking, and he just wants to make it worse. This pollution will cause a disaster, it's already happening. The smoke... it's in the smog. The fumes... they kill...."

The protester was shot down by surrounding policemen. Not an unusual sight these days. An image of the glassy-eyed activist flashed on the screen seconds before they managed to cut back to the studio.

I switched it off, not particularly interested in listening to any more of this scaremongering. I left the rest of my dinner and went up to bed, exhausted from the stress of today.

The week passed by with a regular monotony, but by the next Monday we arrived for registration to find a good third of the class missing. Dozens of people had called in sick, and this wasn't limited to students either. A mask for the mouth and nose sat on each desk, accompanied by a leaflet from Public Health England. It said that the masks were a precautionary measure to prevent seasonal illnesses from spreading.

I looked over at Freddie, asking him what he thought. But he was gazing at his phone, an expression of horror creeping over his face. Peering over his shoulder, we watched as a snarling rabid – like man tore his way through a packed shopping centre in central London. My stomach turned as we saw him run at people, biting and ripping into flesh. Blood spurting in every direction. Then the military came running in, guns blazing and shooting at everyone. The live stream ended abruptly, with the camera clattering to the ground in a burst of static.

By this point the whole form was watching, and a terrified silence hung over the group. What the hell was that man doing? Was it this 'seasonal sickness' they're worried about?

Or was it just some kind of prank?

I had no idea. Thoroughly shaken, the class returned to their seats, each of them lost in thought about what they had just seen. I mean, that couldn't be real, surely not. Some sort of clever CGI trick, probably for a TV show or something, right?

But it wasn't right, something felt wrong, very wrong. The bell rang out and I scraped back my chair, attempting to shake the images of the mauled bodies from my head.

I made my way to my first lesson, meandering around the corridors with the video still weighing heavy on my mind. When I walked into the classroom, everyone was talking about it. People were confused, and probably quite scared too, although no one admitted that.

Time plodded forward, ever slow, until the end of the day. I pulled my phone out of my pocket, trying to find some more information about that video. A bunch of crazy conspiracy theorists were saying that it was a virus released by the government, a very brave claim, other people suggesting that it was just a prank. But then the headline that would change everything flashed at the top of the page. A plane had crashed in Birmingham. At first, I thought nothing of it, but as I scrolled further down the article, that cold sense of dread crept back up my spine.

Videos were emerging of the final few minutes of the flight before the crash – it showed the same thing as the video from the shopping centre. A crazy, snarling man, foaming at the mouth suddenly appeared in the aisle and began mauling bodies, biting and scratching at anyone that came in his path.

He made his way down the plane, gorging on human flesh, blood running in rivers underneath his feet and dripping down his body.

And then the weirdest part – the recovered CCTV from the plane showed the first people that he attacked then stand up, snarling and foaming too, savaging the remaining healthy people. The pilots were overpowered, the flimsy metal door proving no match for these bloodthirsty monsters.

With no one at the helm the plane began to plummet towards the city, exploding in a fireball in the city centre. The zombie – like creatures stumbled on into the city.

I tried to scroll down the page, but the internet cut out

again, so I decided to start walking to the bus stop. Spotting Freddie in the sea of people pouring out of the school gates, I caught up with him, wanting to tell him about the plane crash.

"Hey, did you hear about the plane crash in Birmingham?" I asked, trying to mask the concern in my voice. I really had no idea why I felt so worried about this.

"Good afternoon to you too, Evie!" joked Freddie, but his laughter soon turned to worry as he saw the look on my face.

"I think it was linked to the video that we saw earlier, you know, the one in the shopping centre."

He looked at me, and then laughed.

"You're seriously still worrying about that?" he teased.

"It's probably just some kind of PR stunt for a TV show or something, it isn't anything to be worried about.

No one can get ill and then start eating people like some kind of zombie because that sort of stuff isn't real!"

He was right, I was overthinking everything.

It was all just an elaborate PR stunt, nothing at all to worry about.

I climbed onto the bus and found my seat; the repressive stench of body odour seeping uninvited into my nose. As the bus rumbled into life and drove off, I stared out of the window. A decade of financial crisis had hit this area hard. Kids barefoot in the streets, tents lining the alleyways. People, young and old, just sat on the pavements staring into oblivion because there is no work. A man held a sign, boldly proclaiming "BIOFLEX CAN'T BE TRUSTED. BEWARE OF THE VULCAN CAMPS! FIND THE MISSING!"

These people will do anything for attention. You see them a lot, these days. Conspiracy theorists, looking for someone to blame for the mess that they're in. Who even are BioFlex, anyways? And what on earth is a Vulcan camp?

I got home a few minutes later, exhausted from all the drama of the day to find my mum passed out on the sofa; a bottle of vodka spilling onto the carpet and Jeremy Kyle reruns on the TV. Sighing, I closed the door and headed upstairs, eager to forget about her as well.

I sat at my desk resigned to the fact that I'd better do some homework – my English essay that I was supposed to work on over the summer was due tomorrow and I'd barely even started. My books lay in an uninviting heap on the corner of my desk – something else that I needed to sort out. I opened my computer and got to work on this essay – at least it was an interesting topic to discuss. Writing was my way of switching off from the outside world; I plugged my headphones in and just wrote whatever came to my mind. When my dad disappeared last year, being able to lose myself in imaginary worlds that I constructed was the only thing that kept me from going insane.

Very quickly, I forgot all about the stress and tension of the day as I became lost in the words that were filling my screen.

Hours later I made my way downstairs, starving after finishing my work. I opened the fridge, hoping to find something for dinner. Nothing. My mum was still lying on the sofa, drunk and asleep. The most I found was a slightly soft banana and an out of date Twirl bar. Taking my meagre meal upstairs with me, I decided to go to bed.

Staring into the darkness, I laid on my lumpy mattress and tried to get to sleep. But the images and events of today swam round my mind, filling my head with those grotesque deformations. What were those things?

But I remembered Freddie's words – it wasn't real. It wasn't real. I drifted off to sleep, eager to put the events of today behind me. Tomorrow would be a new day and surely nothing that bad could happen twice in a week, could it?

The next morning, I awoke refreshed and ready to face a new day. I gathered my books and my homework and went downstairs. My mother was sat at the table, a half empty bottle of wine already in her hand.

She attempted to take a drink but missed her mouth entirely, pouring the bottle down her soiled shirt. Cursing angrily, she noticed me staring at her with disgust.

"Who do you think you are, young lady, looking at me like that?" she bellowed, promptly falling over and vomiting as she tried to stand up.

At that point I decided to leave – she could deal with her issues herself. Besides, she's beyond the point of help – she's already half dead.

I walked out of the door as the smell of her vomit began to make me feel nauseous. I got halfway down the street before realising that I'd left my essay at home, but it was too late, I wasn't going back in there.

Finding myself at Freddie's door, I realised that he probably wouldn't even be awake yet. I decided to knock anyway, hoping that his mum might be awake.

The door swung open almost instantaneously and sure enough his mum, Rachel, was standing there.

"My, you're early this morning," she smiled. "Come on in Evie, don't stay out in the cold!"

I followed her in, grateful for the warmth. They were wealthy enough to afford generators to keep them warm when the power goes out... I felt a pang of jealousy.

"So, how're you doing?" she asked. "Everything okay? How's things at home?" Her relentless barrage of questions began to irritate me, but I couldn't show that. "Yeah... things aren't too great at the moment. Mum still hasn't got a job and the drinking has become even worse, this morning she was drinking before she'd even eaten, not that there is anything to eat anyway. She was still so drunk from last night that she spilled it everywhere and then vomited and..." I trailed off, feeling tears pricking my eyelids.

Rachel looked back at me, shocked and aghast at what I told her.

"I'm sorry... I had no idea... I don't know what to say.

If you ever need anything at all, you're always welcome here," she said, with a genuine look of concern on her face.

I smiled at her and asked her if I could possibly have something to eat.

Moments later she returned with a steaming mountain

of eggs, toast and pastries… I wasn't going hungry this morning!

Half an hour later we made our way to school and I filled Freddie in with everything that had happened with my mum.

I was dreading going back home tonight – I knew that there would be nothing to eat and nothing to do except from listen to her scream at me in a drunken range. Oh, and she didn't give me any money to top up the electricity meter so there wouldn't be any warmth or Wi-Fi tonight. Not that it mattered anyway, given the fact that our area never gets electricity anyway.

We arrived at school to see huge tents and fences constructed around the gates – everyone was lining up in front of the tents for some sort of routine virus screening test. But this felt anything but normal. The doctors were dressed in hazmat suits, the word BioFlex stamped on their backs. The name was familiar, but I couldn't put my finger on it. We joined the back of one of the queues as there was no way to skip them and started asking other people what this was all about. People seemed nervous – even though the doctors said that this was just a routine check, nothing to worry about.

But I think people started putting two and two together, everyone had seen the terrifying footage of the shopping centre and the plane crash.

There was a much bigger threat at large.

It was at that moment that the news broke of the latest 'attack' – a new, unidentified virus was sweeping the Northern counties, the areas hit hardest when the health service collapsed.

Videos began emerging on Twitter of crazed, psychotic monsters tearing through towns and villages, infected humans running at healthy residents and slashing them to pieces in pools of blood. But silence from the State News Channel.

Then the internet cut out.

The queue wearily shuffled closer and closer towards the entrance of the tents until I found myself at the front. I was called forwards and hustled into the tent; a torch was shone in my eyes and my cheek was swabbed. I tried to protest but a soldier stepped out of the shadows, gun in hand. A flutter of panic danced in my stomach – what was a soldier doing in the gates of a school? Especially if this was just some kind of routine check, although their method of administration was perhaps a bit on the odd side.

The doctors performed another few tests and took a blood sample, and once their test device flashed green, a muffled voice told me to get out.

What would've happened if the blood monitor didn't go green? What then?

Everything about this seemed so strange, yet they told us nothing and gave us no information as to what was going on.

Freddie came through the tent a few minutes later, and we stood waiting for a few of our other friends. He too did not offer an explanation as to what was going on, but deep down we all knew that whatever this was, whatever was going on, was linked to all these strange videos circulating these past few days.

I was peering into one of the shelters trying to spot our classmates when one of the tents started to flash a bright red. A hush descended around us. A swarm of soldiers rushed towards the tent and moments later someone was dragged out kicking and screaming, bundled into a grey van and driven off.

A surge of children ran forwards, shouting and screaming at the doctors and the soldiers for answers – people wanted to know what was going on.

Freddie and I decided to head inside, finding a seat in

the deserted library. Both of us knew that whatever was going on, whatever this was, it wasn't going to blow over quickly.

Things were getting weirder and weirder by the day; God knows how far this would escalate before this would be over.

And just as things have begun to take sharp turns out of the ordinary, the news and the media have still said nothing about this mysterious virus. I pulled my phone out to check Twitter – the internet was still down.

Maybe I'm just paranoid, or maybe they've shut the internet down so these videos can stop circulating in a drastic attempt to quell mass hysteria... I'm just being paranoid. I think.

As the world celebrated the arrival of 2028, the grey van pulled to a stop outside 25 May Gardens. The men in the boots jumped out in a routine now all too familiar.
"Take them all, that's the order," whispered one of the men.
They cut through the door and ran inside, ready to capture.
A man, one of the residents, began to protest but fell silent when his eyes rested on the guns trained on his forehead.
Moments later, he was sat in the back of the grey van, blindfolded and shackled. One of the other men came back.
"The other two aren't here," he whispered.
The van drove off, leaving the front door of 25 May Gardens swinging limply in the wind.
And still, the world slept.

Chapter Two

The rest of the week passed by fairly uneventfully, there were several more vaccinations to be had and we were made to be screened every morning before entering school. The internet was back – however all mentions or references to the mysterious events that occurred in the past few weeks had vanished – hardly surprising. For the moment things seemed to have settled, although I still haven't gone home. I've been living with Freddie for the past week, I can't face going back to my mum. She knew where I was, but never made any attempt to find or contact me after that. Someone else's problem now, she thinks.

I remember the date it happened well – the 26th of September. I woke up that morning as if it was any other, ready for another day of uneventful lessons. The strange events of the past few weeks behind us, it was as if things were normal again.

I made my way to the first lesson of the day – I had biology and Freddie had art. We went our separate ways and made our way to our classes, unaware of what was to come.

I slipped into a seat at the back of the class and pulled

out my book, not really paying any attention to what the teacher was saying – I hated biology with a passion. I leaned over and whispered something to the guy next to me, George – he erupted into uncontrollable fits of laughter and staggered out of the classroom. The teacher, oblivious to this interruption, droned on unfazed.

The door handle turned, and his face appeared in the window for a split second before this roaring creature hurled himself at him, throwing him on the ground. Thick red blood sprayed up at the window, his screams echoing in the empty corridor through the low growls and roars of this… monster.

The teacher, having only just realised that something was wrong, made his way towards the door. He grasped the door handle, the muscles in his arm tensing as he pulled the door further open. His eyes widened in shock as he saw the monstrosity before him… the sound of his shoes against the cold floor was the only sound in the room as he ran from the door. He was too slow. Grabbing anything that he could find, he hurled whatever he could at this monster. But nothing would stop this beast.

The rest of the class ran out of the back exit and stood watching through the window, but the teacher stayed where he was.

He attempted to stop the creature, he tried to kill it. The sound of his screams as the deformity ripped through his flesh will haunt me till the day I die.

The sight of his blood gushing in torrents across the plastic floor stained in my mind forevermore.

As the mangled carcass of the biology teacher lay twitching on the ground, George stumbled back into the classroom. His eyes rolled back in his head and his jaw slackened, with blood running down his chest from a huge rip in his neck.

"We've got to help him!" yelled a voice from the back of the crowd. "He's going to die! We have to help!!"

I turned around, motioning for them to be quiet but it was too late.

Both him and the original attacker heard the sound and in a split second ran at the windows. They burst through the glass, sending shards flying in all directions.

I ran as fast as I could, fleeing the monstrosities. Some made it away, managing to hide behind trees or bins - others weren't so lucky.

I watched as my classmates, my friends that I've known for years, died and reanimated in front of my eyes.

Screams of anguish and pain could be heard over the top of the roars and growls of the ever-growing horde of zombies... at least that's what I thought they were. There had to be a way to kill them, right?

More and more of my undead friends staggered to their feet, growling and snarling. Some broke away from the main group, meandering aimlessly to destinations unknown.

From my hiding place I watched as their iris - less, bloodshot eyes stared unseeingly into nothingness – They couldn't see me, but they could hear me breathe. I was terrified that I'd make some kind of noise, some kind of signal that would turn them on me.

Trembling, I crept away from the melee and ran away. My mind was reeling from what I had just seen – what HAD I just seen? It suddenly dawned on me that I had no idea what to do now – if I tell someone that there are 'zombies' roaming around, they'll just think I'm mad. Maybe I am mad, maybe this is all just a dream. I pinched my face, just to be certain.

Nope, not a dream. Still very, very real. Still very, very dangerous.

I pulled my phone out, hoping that the internet would provide me with some kind of answer. But the internet was gone again, it had been cut. I tried to phone Freddie – but there was no network connection.

Panic tore through my body, I really had no idea what to do now. Do I run, leaving nature to take its course? Or do I try and warn others somehow?

It was then that my eyes passed over the big red button that I thought could save everyone – the fire alarm. Without due thought or hesitation, I ran up to it and sounded the alarm, hoping that it would draw everyone outside and into a safe area. In hindsight, that plan couldn't have been more flawed. Within a matter of minutes, hundreds of children began pouring out of the buildings and flooded towards the fields – right into the path of the zombies. The shrieks and shouts of children delighted at this unexpected interruption to their lessons morphed into piercing screams as they were mauled by these bloodthirsty, hellish beasts. My stomach turned as the unintended consequences of my actions hit me like a brick.

I killed all of them.

The undead, seemingly emboldened with all this opportunity for fresh meat, ran free amongst the crowd, biting and snarling as more and more of the children dropped dead. Soon, there were more dead than there were alive.

I killed them.

It was then that a sudden realisation smacked me in the face. The world has changed, is changing every second. Society as it is will look totally different within a week, a month, a year.

Now, I had to hunt. Or be hunted.

I ripped a wooden fence spike from the ground, swinging it round into the path of the oncoming undead. Blood and flesh sprayed in all directions; the sickening crunch of breaking bones filled the air. Some of the older kids followed my lead, finding whatever they could to throw or hit with. Teachers and students alike succumbed to the dead.

The deep, distant rumble of a convoy of trucks could be heard over the low groans of the crowd of zombies. They soon came into view, kicking up huge clouds of dust behind them.

"Anybody not infected with the virus, please find shelter immediately. You have 30 seconds. I repeat, anyone not infected with the virus, please find shelter."

His sharp words cut through the chaos, the menacing tone sending shivers down my spine. I ran, knowing full well if I didn't, I'd die.

Crouching behind a building, I glanced over at the trucks. They were emblazoned with the BioFlex insignia, a name I'd grown to distrust over the past few weeks. Something just didn't feel right about this. How did they know to turn up just as things got bad? Were they watching, somehow?

I had no idea. The knot of unease in my stomach tightened as I saw kids stood rooted to the spot, unable to move.

I could only watch with horror as the BioFlex soldiers began machine-gunning down the crowd, killing everything in their line of sight irrespective of whether or not they were infected.

Their merciless torrent of bullets continued to fly until there was no one left standing. The soldier came back out, demanding that anyone else still alive make their way into the back of one of the trucks.

Shaken, I followed the instruction – I had no idea what they were going to do next, so their side seemed safest. And I was right.

The trucks began to roll out almost instantly, thundering back towards the road. I looked round at the faces that lined the cold, metal benches – each of them stared back at me with fearful, panicked eyes.

Most of them were so small – not much older than 12 years old. No one spoke; the silence that hung heavy through the air was only punctuated by the occasional sniffle and the relentless thundering of the engine. The harrowing images of their classmates being slaughtered like animals were burned onto their retinae. In that moment, their innocence was snatched from them like an autumn leaf in the wind. They had been exposed to the true colours of the new world.

But if they were to survive this, they're going to have to get a lot tougher. One of the children tapped me on the arm, looking up nervously.

"Do you know where we're going?" she half whispered, her voice catching as if on the verge of tears.

I turned around and looked at her, smiling sadly.

"No, I don't, but I'm sure they're taking us somewhere safe. We'll be alright, don't worry."

She looked up at me, whispered a thank you and turned back away.

The convoy of trucks suddenly pulled to a screeching stop, jolting everyone back to life. I stood up and peered out of the small windows and spotted our school in the distance. There wasn't much else around, just a deserted motorway. As I turned to look away, there was a blinding flash in the general direction of our school followed by a dull 'boom' sound. A bomb. They had bombed the school.

That's when I knew – things were now very, very, bad. I mean, an isolated outbreak of zombies (that still didn't feel right to say!) was terrifying and just wrong on so many levels – but bombs? This felt like a coordinated response, as if this was some kind of protocol. But my earlier question was still unanswered – how did these 'BioFlex' people know how to get to the school so quickly?

It was almost as if it was… planned?

No. That's ridiculous.

My thoughts were interrupted by the BioFlex soldiers who had flung the doors at the back of lorry wide open. A skinny man clutching a microphone popped up from the back of his truck and proceeded to speak.

"As the Biological Warfare Division of the British Army, it is our duty to protect you and inform you. The UK has been the subject of a biological weapon attack, causing a new virus to spread. We do not know what this is or how to cure it, so affected areas are under mandatory evacuation. Your school was an infected area, so containment protocols were engaged."

His eyes settled on the smouldering piles of rubble that

was previously a vast educational complex.

"As you were all in an infected hotspot, you are required by law to attend a mandatory infection screening at the temporary military hospital." He began to turn away as one of the older kids yelled at him.

"What law? You have no legal authority over me – I know because I'm studying Law," he sang in a horrendously smug manner.

I had no idea. I had no idea what was going to happen to any of us. The question at the forefront of my mind, however, was this - could we really trust these guys?

They never introduced themselves as part of the Army just part of the 'infection control' team at the school gates all those weeks ago, and there was nothing on their uniforms to suggest this either.

Clearly, someone else was having similar thoughts as me. One boy jumped out of one of the other trucks and tried to run off.

"I'm not going anywhere with you lot! You're just going to kill us – you don't want to help," he yelled, tears streaming down his face. His long hair blew in the wind as he stood there shaking, refusing to move.

"We have been authorized to shoot anyone that does

not comply with our instructions. If you do not get back in that truck right now, we will shoot." The soldier glared at him, anger emanating from his eyes.

"I'm going nowhere." The boy was calm now. I'd rather die than live through this."

A hush descended on the crowd of schoolchildren. Even the soldier looked visibly shaken – he hadn't expected a response in that vein, and certainly not one with that level of confidence and certainty. The boy raised his hands and locked eyes with the soldier. Gazing coolly at the gun, the tension that filled the air seemed tangible enough to touch.

The silence was sickening.

At a guess, the soldier that was supposed to shoot him was only a few years older than me. Barely an adult, yet here he stands, playing God with someone's life.

I didn't think that he was going to do it. For a moment, I honestly thought that the soldier didn't have it in him. He seemed so small, so weak. Yet, with a twitch of his finger, he was instantly the stronger man. The boy dropped to the ground as a burst of bullets ripped through his chest. Shattering the silence, the shots echoed across the empty road. A single gasp, then his eyes rolled back in his head. Dead.

The grey trucks were filled with forgotten souls. Rows and rows of these trucks began to line up, each of them identical. Their contents – a burden on society. The undesirables. The outspoken. The disabled.

More men in boots arrive. They stand, their backs to the trucks. We see their helmets, the word VULCAN printed in bold lettering. The sweeping glare of the searchlights illuminates the scale of this operation.

And still, the world sleeps.

Chapter Three

The dead body lay crumped and unmoving; dark pools of blood stained the tarmac road beneath him. The BioFlex soldier turned around and hopped back into one of the trucks, whistling nonchalantly as if nothing had happened. But for the rest of us, that moment would haunt us forever. The small gasp as the bullet pierced his chest. The way his eyes rolled back. How his had body slackened and crumpled.

The trucks rumbled back into life and began thundering down the road, taking us ever closer to our seemingly new lives. The sun began to slowly sink into the ground, the final faint beams of light a beacon of hope in the all – encompassing gloom of our current predicament. Save for the monotony of the engines, the world was quiet. The birds were silent, the roads empty.

So, where the hell was everyone? And did they know what we know?

But as we drove further and further out from the town and closer to our new lives, it became clear that we weren't getting any more answers, not now.

Over the next few hours, I drifted in and out of fitful

sleep as the truck ploughed onwards.

Images of the past few days cut through my dreams, a constant reminder of how everything has changed.

Several hours had passed and the night wore on. Most of the kids had managed to drift into a light slumber… but I couldn't. Every time I closed my eyes I could just see – well, you know what I can see.

Thunder rumbled in the distance as rain began to strafe the sides of the truck. It's been raining every day for the past thirty days, and when it's not raining, it's boiling – climate change gone mad. The floods have been bad too – thankfully not where we lived though.

Water began to trickle down my back, through the sides of the truck, as the rain continued to hammer down. The truck pulled to an abrupt stop and bright lights dazzled us as they pulled the doors open.

"Everybody out, quickly. Get into lines and don't talk," barked the soldier, clearly grumpy at being sent out into the pouring rain. The kid next to me grabbed my hand and whispered in my ear, asking if his mum was here.

I had no idea, but I knew sure as hell that this kid would never see his mum again as long as he lived.

We stepped out of the truck and into the rain, finding a queue to join.

I gazed upwards as I took in my surroundings – there were hundreds of other trucks parked up, and miles of fencing, topped with barbed wire, stretching off into the distance. The compound was illuminated with glaring white floodlights, bathing the vicinity in a clinical, cold light. And the building behind all of this was even more impressive – a vast stadium that just didn't seem to stop, stretching for miles in each direction. This looked like they were prepared for the worst.

Trucks kept pulling up, each of them filled up with kids like us. No one really knew what was going on – some kids had no idea about the whole 'zombie' situation that we seem to have on our hands – they thought that this was to do with the flood crisis rather than any other apocalyptic virus.

They refused to accept what I told them – the most dangerous thing to do is believe what the soldiers tell you. They were told that they were perfectly safe, they were just being evacuated because of a flood risk. Others were told that it's because of the 'dirty air.'

Everyone's been told something different. There was a palpable tension in the air as everyone was confused and panicked as to what was going on and some of the smaller children had been crying non-stop for the past hour.

"OI! What the hell do you think you're doing? Give me back my bag! Don't you touch me, I swear…"
A fight had broken out, and the kids surged forwards to get a look in at the action. The surrounding soldiers did nothing, they just carried on registering the children who were in their lines.

The two boys must have been around 17, and the crowd looked on in bewilderment as they fought. The screams and grunts of frustration of both boys filled the air as they tussled on the ground, each of them alternately bashing each other in the face, in the gut, wherever. Then one of them, the bigger of the two, hauled himself to his feet and raised his head above his opponent's head. With an animalistic roar, he smashed his boot into the head of the guy on the floor, sending blood spraying into the crowd.
He killed him, and no one did a thing.
Not one of the soldiers turned their heads.
The crowd fell silent.
We carried on moving forwards in our lines, the rain soaking us to the bone. I reached the front of the queue and was given a change of clothes in exchange for my name and address. I joined a group of people waiting to be escorted inside and searched in the sea of faces for Freddie, but he was nowhere to be seen.

———

The soldier at the front of our group instructed us to move forward, imploring us to stay within the cold glare of the floodlights. As we moved towards the compound, I looked behind me towards the fence. Trucks and busses continued to pull up with swathes of kids pouring through the gates. But not a single adult, save for the soldiers around us.

The great steel doors opened with a hiss, revealing a vast military complex spanning as far as the eye could see. Worried - looking scientists with the words "BioFlex Outbreak Team" emblazoned on their backs rushed back and forth; soldiers with rifles slung over their shoulders marched past constantly.

We were escorted to a vast hall full of thousands of other children all sitting along wooden benches in an uncomfortable quiet.

A small boy, probably no older than five or six, grabbed my hand and asked me where he could find his mother.

I bent down to talk to him and told him that I had no idea, but one of the soldiers saw me speak. He walked over - unease started to build in my stomach.

"NO TALKING," he roared in my face.

The boy next to me started to cry, desperate for the comfort of his mother. Incensed, the soldier spun round again and slapped him across the face, screaming at him to be quiet.

That didn't go down well.

"What the hell do you think you're doing? He's a bloody child!"

One of the kids pulled a knife from his pocket. The other two exchanged a glance, agreeing that this wasn't going to end well.

"Jeremey... put the knife away. He'll kill you," they whispered to him.

But Jeremey refused to listen, hellbent on avenging the little boy. His arm shot forwards plunging the knife towards the soldier's abdomen, which bounced straight off his reinforced uniform.

Without a thought, the solider raised his gun and shot Jeremey squarely between the eyes. His body dropped and crumpled as an audible gasp spread across the hall.

What manner of things has gone so wrong that the military has resorted to massacring innocent children?

The rest of us quietly filed towards the checkpoint at the front of the hall. We were asked for our names and address again, and then they asked us to give them our hand. They stamped a number on each child – that's all we are now, a number. I made my way down to the benches in the main hall with the small boy still in tow and found the bench for our numbers.

I sat, finally alone with my thoughts. I thought of Freddie, I thought of my mum. Where were they? Has the government informed the outside world of this apocalyptic situation? And who the hell were BioFlex? BioFlex... the name stirred a memory from long ago, something to do with the military.

That's when it hit me. It was the organization that the government sold off the armed forces to when they privatized the military. And it was a BioFlex compound that blew up all those weeks ago on the news.

This was all starting to sound like a farfetched conspiracy theory... it's probably just a coincidence. But my thoughts were loudly interrupted by the obnoxious blaring of an alarm.

One of the soldiers started barking at us to stand, instructing us to move out of the hall bench by bench. Our bench was one of the last to leave; we stood and walked silently towards our new lives.

We were walking for what seemed an eternity until at last we came to a stop. The guard punched a code into a keypad and a door swung open, revealing a cramped room with sleeping bags laid out in ordered rows on the floor. They tried to cram at least fifty of us into a room that really only fits about ten... I opened my mouth to protest but then remembered what happened to Jeremey earlier on.

All I knew is that somehow, I had to get out of here. We entered the room one by one, the first few people taking the comfortable positions against the wall or in the corner. By the time I made it in there, the area by the toilet was one of the last spaces left. Penned in like animals.

The guard at the door addressed us, telling us that we are not to leave this room save for our hour of exercise a day and for our three meals. It's as if we were criminals. But even prisoners don't get this sort of treatment.

This is more akin to a prison camp.

But the irony of this thought wouldn't become apparent for months to come.

Children sat crying, rocking back and forth, whilst others had already drifted off to sleep. I just sat staring at the wall, unblinking and unthinking. Sleep wouldn't take me until the small hours of the morning... my thin, scratchy sleeping bag providing little comfort in this darkness.

*Van by van, those grey metal doors swung open.
Blindfolded and shackled, the prisoners were led out. One
by one, they knelt on the cold, wet floor. The grass was light
with dew, an earthy scent filling the air.
The air was still, save for the hum of generators and the
occasional bird.
Now devoid of their cargo, the vans began to pull away. The
Vulcans remained standing to attention, watching over
their prisoners. No one moved, no one said a word.
The floodlights behind us illuminated the true horror
behind us for the first time. Bathed in white, a true
dystopian nightmare stretched into the horizon.
For decades, they said, "It could never happen here!"
Oh, how wrong were they.
And still, the world slept.*

Chapter 4

The metallic door penning us in swung open with a clang, startling me out of my fitful slumber. I sat up, momentarily confused as to where I was. Then it all came back to me, the whirlwind that was the past few days. There was already a queue for the bathroom and we'd only been up a minute.

I knew something for sure – we had to escape, no matter what – I'd rather die out there at the hand of some infected monster than in here.

Rolling my mat away, I stood up and headed for the door. My mouth was drier than sandpaper and my stomach longed for some proper food. I tried to leave, but the guard stopped me.

Not until everyone's ready, he said.

They weren't going to be ready for a while. I slumped against a wall, wishing I could just be at home in peace. Wishing I had Freddie with me.

But home, Freddie, privacy – all gone. This was my life now.

"Hey." A voice next to me whispered in my ear. I turned towards it, not really in the mood for talking.

"What do you want," I asked him.

"I know a way out." My stomach dropped; my heart started racing. I needed to hear what he had to say.

But at that moment, the guard told us that it's time to go. Walk in silence, we were instructed. We walked down the corridors, the only sound our shoes echoing off the cold metal walls. Identical doors lined the path, all of them presumably holding groups of children.

The canteen came into view as we rounded the corner, a stark contrast to the rest of the building. A low, fervent chatter filled the air. The smell of bread and porridge was a welcome change from the sickening blend of body odour and bleach in the rest of the building. I grabbed a tray and lined up to get my serving.

A ladle of grey sludge was slopped onto my tray and a piece of dry toast tossed on top. I looked down in disappointment at the food; to be fair I wasn't expecting anything much better. The guy who started talking to me just before we left looked equally miffed as he followed me to a table. He hunched over the table, careful not to let anyone hear what he was about to say. "Listen. I can get us out. I know the guard assigned to our room. He hates it here too but can't leave. He told me how to get out – are you with me?"
 He stared with an almost unhinged intensity into my eyes.

I mean I can't say that I had my doubts. Sceptical at best, I found myself agreeing to escape, well aware that this could cost me my life.

"Okay. We have to bide our time; we'll get out when the next batch of children arrive to be processed. Be ready."

My heart sank, I was hoping we'd get out of this prison today. He saw the look on my face and subsequently explained that our escape route is left unguarded when they're distracted processing the new kids.

"I'm Everest, by the way."

"Evie."

"Nice to meet you, Evie." He grinned, before adding;

"Wish it could've been in nicer circumstances though."

I nodded in agreement and continued to pick at my slimy porridge wordlessly, my stomach occasionally heaving at the taste.

Breakfast finished and we made our way back to the room. In our absence, a change of clothes, a toothbrush and some blankets had been laid out, as well as a selection of games to pass the time.

It was something, I guess. I spotted a game of Monopoly – I loved that game when I was younger. I always won.

They'd also left a stack of books for the older kids –

nothing decent though since the Literary Purge removed anything grounded in political protest.

The 2020s were a dark time in British history.

I searched through the stack and found a dog – eared copy of Harry Potter. Letting the words wash over me, I detached from my plight and relaxed.

Miles and miles of barbed wire and chain – link fencing
stretched as far as the eye could see. Huge concrete watch
towers stood over every corner, an ever – present, all seeing
eye. Rows and rows of huts filled the centre space, the rest,
just emptiness. A vast emptiness. Sweeping searchlights
illuminated lines of prisoners being led to the front gates,
the captives fading into the darkness as the light moved on.
A metallic scraping filled the air as the great iron gates
moved to let them pass.

They'd never see those gates open for them again.

Freddie

I knew I had to keep moving, that much was certain. I'd managed to survive out here for the past few weeks, but every day was getting harder.

People out here are already going mad and its only been a short time since this mess started. Every supermarket has been well and truly emptied. People fight in the aisles for the last few tins and bottles of water. Dead bodies litter the streets, the stench of corpses overpowering. So far, I've been able to fend off the Soulless (yes, that's what I'm calling the zombies) with my limited arsenal of weapons, but what I really want is a baseball bat. Preferably metal, maybe with barbed wire like that guy from the zombie TV show. Looks pretty badass if you ask me.

I was searching through an abandoned office block earlier, trying to work out if it was a decent place to set up camp when I came across a group of survivors. They told me that there are camps we can go to; the army keep you safe there.

I wasn't sure, but they gave me a map of how to get there anyways. But if it was so safe, why didn't they go?

But then again, maybe they took Evie there during the

evacuation? I didn't make it onto the trucks when they evacuated the school.

I'll never forget the sound of those trucks driving off and carrying Evie away... it felt like someone ripped my heart out of my chest. But that's what you need to be in this new world. An emotionless monster.

I had to kill my mum last week. She was bitten by one of the Soulless. Her one wish was that she didn't suffer, she didn't want to become one of them. It was the hardest thing I've done in my life. I couldn't bury her, I had to leave her at the side of the road under a sheet. Every time I think about it, the pain sweeps through my chest like an inferno.

I heard a noise at the front of the building. Adrenaline coursed through my veins as I jumped to my feet, clutching my knife. I'd fashioned it into a sort of bayonet, welding it onto a metal pole to attack from distances.

Peering around the corner, my heart hammered in my chest. I was convinced it was so loud it was going to give me away... this was terrifying.

A crowd of the Soulless were banging on the metal shutters.

Their raspy breathing intensified as I got closer; unease and fear crept up my spine like an icy chill.

It was a sizeable crowd, but I reckoned I could dispatch them easily enough.

Putting my emotions aside, I got to work, stabbing with my makeshift bayonet through the shutters.

Blood spurted in all directions as they began to drop one by one until just a handful remained.

Then something went very wrong. I pulled the knife back it didn't come. It made a horrendous grinding noise as the bayonet got stuck in the metal shutter, undoubtedly attracting more of the Soulless. I pulled it again and the shutters gave a sickening lurch forwards before crashing to the ground. The sound attracted every Soulless in a mile – they all came bounding over with a sense of energy that I'll never quite comprehend.

A primitive instinct kicked in – I ran as fast as I could towards the back of the building but stopped dead in my tracks as I realised there was a breach there too. Like a mouse in a trap, I was well and truly stuck. Nausea crept up my throat as I stumbled backwards, tripping onto a clothes rail.

Now defenceless against the oncoming hordes of the Soulless, I realised that the metal poles of the clothes rails would make weapons strong enough for me to maybe, just maybe, get out of here alive.

With superhuman strength, I ripped the bars apart and charged into battle with a pole in each hand.

Swinging the bars above my head, blood, brains and guts painted the walls red as the stomach – turning sound of the smashing of skulls drowned out the rasping of the Soulless.

I moved down the corridor like a swimmer floundering against the tide, well aware that I was fighting a battle of life and death on two fronts in a narrow corridor.

Not ideal by any stretch of the imagination!

I kept moving forwards, my arms burning with fatigue, but I couldn't stop. Rest could come later, but for now all I had to focus on was survival. Ploughing forwards like a machine with slain Soulless piling up around me, I was starting to feel a hint of confidence.

I wondered if Evie had to do any of this.

I thought that this was almost over, ready to plan my escape, when the final few of the Soulless stumbled towards me.

Through their miserable grey pallor, I could make out their faces.

My friends. Inseparable since they were born, now bound together in brotherhood even after death. But their unseeing eyes couldn't see their friend, all they saw was food. Tears cut tracks through my grimy cheeks as the metal smashed through their skulls, their blood and brains spraying in every direction.

I slumped against a wall, feeling decidedly miserable. I needed to be stronger than this, emotions are for the weak.

Emotions will kill you. Running back to the room where I'd been hiding, I hastily gathered up my things and threw them into my bag.

I'd decided that I would follow the map to the military base – right now, this seemed like my best chance of survival.

The door swung open with a screech, sending a bolt of panic through my chest. But the coast was clear – no Soulless appeared. I meandered down the high street, bloody bars in hand. One thing was certain – I needed to find a better weapon.

There was a sports shop at the end of the street – I might find my baseball bat in there.

The doors were wide open and there were no signs of any Soulless around; I tentatively stepped inside, my shoes crushing the broken glass underfoot. Surprisingly, the shop was relatively untouched by looters – time to stock up on clothes and shoes. I had a long journey ahead of me.

And then right above the checkout, on the highest shelf, lay the holy grail. The very reason for my quest into the sports shop – the baseball bat. But this wasn't going to be easy – the ladder lay in a mangled heap of metal on the floor. Looks like they used it to bust the till open. Creative.

I decided that the easiest course of action would be to try and pull the shelves down and just collect it like a snack from a vending machine.

With a Tarzan – like leap, I latched onto the shelf and pulled it down on top of me with an almighty crash. I rolled out of the way, narrowly avoiding a huge metal plate to the head. After fighting off hundreds of zombies, it would've been a shame to die at the hands of a shelf.

I pulled my treasure from the wreckage and ripped it out of the packaging. The cold metal felt powerful in my hands – with this, I am invincible.

I swung it round, smashing the plastic head of a dummy into smithereens. Grinning, I felt a sense of happiness wash over me for the first time in weeks – I was safer now.

A Soulless stumbled up the street, picking up its pace as it smelt me. I walked over to it, bat swinging ferociously. The metal tore into the skull effortlessly, sending the creature flying backwards.

One final happy customer for the sports shop.

I pulled out my map and began my journey to the military base. Safety was only a day's walk away.

"Name and address," barked the soldier.

"Uhh…um… Steve Yard, 25 May Gardens." Our prisoner looks up, terrified and confused. "Please…" he whispered. "I have a wife; I have a daughter. Let me go." He pleaded with the soldier at the gate, but he took no notice.

"PLEASE!" he screamed, fresh tears rolling down his face. "LET ME GO!"

A buzz of radio chatter. Heavy boots on concrete. Crack. Steve Yard slumped to the ground, blood trickling down his forehead. Forgotten, disappeared.

One of the men dragged his body in the direction of a small outhouse. A thin, spindly line of blood marked a path in the dirt, the last evidence that this man ever existed.

Evie

A couple of weeks had passed relatively peacefully, although the stench in our cell was becoming unbearable - these kids really needed a shower. Everest hadn't said a word to me since he let me in on his plan to escape; not that I care anyway, I certainly prefer my own company.

The younger kids had kept themselves entertained with the selection of games – a monopoly game had been going all night and showed no signs of stopping.

But underneath all of this, there was a palpable tension in the atmosphere, a growing restlessness. We haven't been outside in days, no one has showered since we got here. And everyone is hungry – there was nowhere near enough food to go around.

Looking round the room, I came to the sobering realisation that I couldn't leave all these children behind to their fate. If I was going to get out, they were going to have to come with me.

But how? Some of them could barely talk! The older kids could make good fighters... but the burden of having to feed them all would be too much.

Regardless, I was going to have to make it work – I couldn't leave them all behind.

Everest wasn't going to like this.

Anyway – I don't even know the state of the world out there, for all I know they've managed to fix everything, cured all of the infected and then we can go home safely. But deep down I knew that the world outside was a different one to the weeks before.

I picked my way across the room, stepping delicately over the children slumped across the floor until I reached Everest.

"We have to take them with us. I… we can't leave them here. They'll die."

He turned to me with a look of derision.

"And how in God's name do you think we're going to bust 40 plus kids out of here? And what about the kids in the other cells - there's thousands of them in here. We can't take them all! Just you, and me.

I had a plan to get us out. All of us.

Later that day, the guard returned to collect us for dinner. I noticed the machine gun slung across his back – my stomach turned with adrenaline as I prepared to enact my grand plan. Everest and I lined up to collect our trays, ready for action.

All at once, we turned around and slammed the metal trays into the guard directly behind us.

He slumped to the floor as his skull made a sickening squelching sound. Seconds later, his bloodshot eyes rolled back in his mangled head. I ripped his machine gun off his back and immediately started firing at the other soldiers around the room. Before they even registered what was happening, they began to fire back. But for them, it was too late. A handful of other kids had taken guns from fallen soldiers and began shooting them down. Before long, the motley child army had captured the cafeteria and assumed control. The bodies of fallen soldiers hung dramatically from the balconies and the crudely constructed makeshift barricades.

After days of quiet and misery, there was a jubilant atmosphere amongst the young militia.

I jumped onto one of the tables and began addressing my ragtag army.

"We've now established control of this side of the building. But this is a huge compound and there's going to be hundreds more of them arriving any second. We need to arm ourselves – if you can find a gun, use it. If not, break the table legs and use the poles to batter them.

We're going to barricade the central corridor – they will have nowhere to go. And then we will be free!"

I barely finished talking before the crowd erupted into raucous applause and cheers – they were ready to fight for their freedom.

The thundering of boots echoed down the corridor. We hid behind our barricade, ready to fight. My heart thundered in my chest as I hoisted my gun above the barricade.

They were here.

"ATTACK!" I bellowed. Bullets flew in every direction, the narrow corridor proving fatal for the soldiers. Line by line they fell, dead and dying.

Our table – leg division was hard at work at the back of the flank of soldiers, dispatching them like machines with a blow to the back of the head. Before long, they all lay dead in the corridor.

But the casualties weren't limited to their side – dozens of our children lay dead, slumped over our barricade like revolutionaries.

A piercing scream interrupted my thoughts.

"INFECTED!!" bellowed someone in the distance.

A door somewhere must've been breached. I sprinted down the corridor, ready to fight again.

Cautiously, I peered around the corner, noticing a gentle chink of light as a door swung in the wind. The Infected stumbled through, heading towards us.

It would be better to just seal the door and save our ammunition rather than defend the building that kept us captive.

Or, even better, evacuate all the children and then let the Infected roam free around the building – the government can't use it then.

I crept backwards and made my way to the fight.

Everest and I led the children towards the vast entrance atrium. The door still opened – at least they didn't lock down the building. With a metallic hiss, the outside world was revealed to us once more. The light blinded us; we staggered into the sunshine shielding our eyes.

It looks like the guards outside caught wind of the coup inside and ran. We walked up to the gates which were swinging gently in the breeze and made our way towards the trucks that took us away from our lives and into this brave new world.

Everest and I had decided to try and make it to France, for several reasons. Mainly because it was one of the last remaining democracies in Europe, since most of the Continent fell to either the Communists or the Fascists in the wake of the post – Brexit break-up of the EU.

And they were one of our few allies in the European

War.

We also didn't know for sure if this outbreak was global – if it was just limited to England, maybe we would be safe there. The kids started filing into the trucks, but I realised I needed drivers for the other dozen trucks or so. A handful of the older kids volunteered themselves, claiming to be able to drive – we didn't have time to debate. I hastily informed them of our plan to make it to the ports and told them to follow our truck.

The convoy rumbled into life and made its way towards the road. The motorway was eerily deserted, not a car in sight. The reason for this rapidly became apparent. The military had blockaded the road. A crude fence had been constructed across the carriageway and a couple of soldiers stepped out. I wasn't stopping. Slamming my foot onto the accelerator, the truck barrelled through the fences and crushed the soldiers effortlessly.

Undoubtedly stirred into action by this sudden commotion, a dozen more BioFlex soldiers poured out of the hut, ready to attack. Clearly, they didn't realise that we were the rescued children from the base.

Our truck shot across their roadblock but no one else made it. I looked behind me in the mirror and saw the other trucks explode into a ball of flames.

Hundreds of children, dead.

But now isn't the time for emotion, emotions are for the weak. They'll kill you out here.

A military radio cracked into life beside me.

"Reported attacks at BioFlex Base 5, 6 and 9. Vulcan 07 has fallen. All personnel in the area report to these designated areas at once. Stop the trucks at all costs. I repeat. Stop the trucks."

Everest and I sat in a stunned silence, quietly absorbing the knowledge that there were at least ten other BioFlex military sites holding people... were they all full of children like us?

I really didn't trust these people.

We drove on in our truck, one locked and loaded keeping watch and the other driving. I was amazed at how empty the motorway was, it was almost as if this whole thing was planned?

I cursed as I spotted another BioFlex roadblock ahead. They were clearly ready for us.

This was a BioFlex truck though. So surely, being a military vehicle, it would have some sort of defence mechanism?

Frantically, I searched across the dashboard until I found what I was looking for.

A small, innocent looking button marked 'ROCKET'
Without hesitation, I pressed it. Nothing happened. I
panicked, thinking that it had failed. Seconds later, an
almighty explosion blasted the roadblock out of the
way in a vast fireball.

Success. I grinned as we ploughed through the
wreckage, confident that we could overcome anything.
We were finally approaching Dover. I called through
to the back of the truck, letting the kids know that we
were almost there. I could see the sea!

We turned off the motorway towards the port. My
heart sank in an instant. We were greeted with the sight
of the most heavily fortified military defence you could
imagine, crawling with soldiers and complete with
machine guns mounted on watch towers. My little
rocket atop the truck was no match for these monsters.
Helicopters circled overhead and huge searchlights
would keep watch in the night. We were not getting
through this.

I had no clue what we were going to do now. Turning
to Everest, he was just as clueless as me. Too late. We
had been spotted. A couple of soldiers walked up to the
truck – if they realised that it was a BioFlex truck, we
were going to be in for some trouble.

I thrust the vehicle into reverse, ploughing through the
oncoming soldiers.

People had noticed the commotion and came running over – we had to get out, quickly.

I wondered if the truck has a machine gun too. And would you believe it, it did! The truck opened fire onto the crowd, keeping the swathe of soldiers at bay. Having bought us an escape, we floored it back towards the motorway. I had absolutely no idea where we were going – anywhere but here.

We were just about in the clear when, in a fraction of a second, the truck screeched to a halt and flipped forwards.

The only sound I could hear was the hissing of the engine – was it going to blow? I had to get out. Disentangling myself from my seatbelt, I looked over at Everest. He was slumped unconscious, blood trickling down the side of his head.

I could smell smoke. The engine was on fire. Hastily, I pulled the machine gun from Everest's hands and climbed out of the truck, wincing as I put pressure on my leg. It felt broken, but I couldn't stop. Somehow, I needed to get Everest out – thankfully his door swung open with little resistance.

I managed to haul him from the wreckage and dragged him onto the side of the road.

The smell of smoke from the engine was getting

stronger... I didn't have long left to get the children out. Wrestling with the door, I realised that the door mechanism had jammed in the crash.

The front of the truck was now engulfed in flames. I had seconds until the whole truck blew. With a final kick, the door opened with an ear - splitting screech. I stepped back to allow the kids to jump down, but they couldn't climb up the slippery truck floor – the back of the truck was pointing upwards after the crash.

The screams of pain and anguish that filled my ears will stay with me until the day I die. I was only stood there for a few seconds, yet it felt like an eternity. Powerless I watched as the truck exploded into a ball of flames, the flames snatching souls with a hazy dance.

I walked round to Everest and slumped down onto the grass.

The fire raged behind me – I couldn't bear to watch. It made me feel responsible, it made me feel like I killed those children. Every single one of those kids we rescued was dead within hours. Maybe we should've left them there, maybe we shouldn't have left at all.

Regret for the past wasn't going to get me anywhere now though. Darkness was beginning to fall. The icy tendrils of the night were beginning to weave their way through the trees, the setting sun filling me with dread and fear.

We had nowhere to go.

If we stay here, we're in danger. If we move, we die.

One by one they filed into their huts; their wrists shackled and their mouths silent. No one dared speak; a palpable terror hung over the room. A child rocked back and forth on their knees, tears silently rolling down their cheeks as the room filled.

A cold wind blew through the building, the flimsy windows rattling and whistling. The beds, tightly packed in rows, were small and uncomfortable. Overhead, a single harsh fluorescent light hummed, bathing the room in a clinical white.

People sat on their assigned beds, legs swinging nervously as they looked around, shell-shocked, unsure what to do next.

The world slept on.

Freddie

I had been walking for what felt like months. My entire body felt like it was on fire – both from exhaustion and the countless nettles that swiped with their innocent venom. Though it has to be said, after a few weeks on the road, my Soulless dispatching skills were now second to none. The novelty of the baseball bat still hasn't worn off – there's no way any zombie is going to take me down so long I have this in my hand.

My stomach rumbled agonisingly; I hadn't eaten properly all day. I'd manage to survive off a limited diet of berries and the occasional rabbit, I felt so, so sick after not having decent food for the past couple of weeks. And I'd been rationing my water; I felt a certain sense of desperation as I realised that my bottle was yet again almost empty.

The journey had been slow so far. I managed to walk miles in the wrong direction – there was no one to rescue me out here! And even though I doubt that there is a cellular service anymore, my phone died along the way so the only real form of security I had was gone too. But that no longer mattered – we were on the home straight now. According to the map, I needed to get off the motorway right about now.

I meandered up the slip road towards the main road – this should take me directly to the military base.

What was I going to find? Will my friends be here? Evie… is she here?

God, I hoped so. I missed her more than you could imagine.

There it was. In all of its miserable glory sat the military compound. Galvanised by this sight, I started to run. But as I drew closer, I realised that something wasn't quite right here. No, something was clearly very wrong. The giant steel gates that once protected the entrance to the compound lay battered and useless on the ground. Burnt – out carcasses of busses and trucks sat limp and lifeless on the concrete plaza, a distinct acrid stench of burning flesh hanging heavy over the whole cold, lifeless landscape.

As I picked my way through the rubble and ruin towards the entrance, I could hear a faint snarling sound. Soulless. Instinctively reaching for my bat, I got ready to attack.

Glancing to my left, I cursed under my breath as my eyes rested on a growing cluster of the Soulless.

There were far too many of them for me to take on alone, especially with my bat. There were discarded guns around me, but the noise would just attract more. I had a split second to make a decision. I decided to run.

And then they all followed.

The shrill ring of a bell stirs the inmates from their slumber. Prisoner 01 sat up abruptly, rubbing their eyes as they realised where they were.

The door swung open as a Vulcan guard marched in. Instructing the prisoners to make their way to the central canteen, another two guards came in behind him. Wordlessly, they grabbed the man on the bed closest to the door and dragged him away, blindfolding him with the same hessian sacks. A scream. A struggle.

A disappearance.

British Government COBRA Meeting

Prime Minister Charlie McIntosh took his seat at the centre of the table, flanked by his security detail and other senior Change Britain politicians. A tense silence hung over the room as the rest of the Cabinet members seated themselves.

Impatiently, he banged his fist on the table, demanding to be updated on the spread of the virus.

The Minister for Public Health stood up first and began to speak, informing the room that the virus was spreading at a rate faster than anticipated. He went on to say that latest estimations predict that 50% or more of the British public has now been infected, and that significant chunks of the country have now been wiped out entirely.

A satisfied grin was beginning to appear at the corner of the Prime Minister's mouth.

A representative of the Ministry of Information then stood. He spoke of how the Ministry has urged all of those yet unaffected by the virus to make their way to government rescue camps, where they will be transported to more permanent safe zones. And anyone that doesn't comply will be shot or left to fend for themselves against the infected.

Then, from a shadowy corner, another voice spoke. His cold words sliced across the room, informing the Prime Minister that the Vulcan prison camps, the other camps, were filling faster than anticipated, and that he needs confirmation to begin the final phase sooner than anticipated.

'Kill them all,' the Prime Minister responded.

One by one, the prisoners lined up to be served. A cold bowl of porridge landed on their trays. Vulcan soldiers patrolled the lines, batons in hand to quell any trouble. A low chatter filled the room, punctuated with the clattering of cutlery against the metal bowl.

A shout interrupted the monotony.

"I WANT PROPER BLOODY FOOD!"

Soldiers flood into the building, guns cocked and ready to fire. He dropped to his knees, an expression of pure horror washing over his face.

"I'm sorry, I'm sorry," he whispered, tears streaming down his eyes.

Too late. Bullets spray, staining his white gown a dark red. His body flew backwards, landing on the dusty floor in a growing pool of blood.

And still, the world slept.

Rachael

I couldn't breathe. I struck outwards, but my hands just flailed uselessly in the crushing darkness. My breath came short and ragged under the hessian hood, and the silence was oppressive. I tried again without success to free myself from my shackles, slicing through the soft flesh around my wrists. Blood trickled down my hands, tickling my fingertips.

The truck jolted violently as we hit what I assumed to be a pothole, although our destination was still a mystery. The last thing I remember was some soldiers on our doorstep… now I'm here.

Breathe. In. Out. In. Out. In. Out. I tried to calm myself down, but I could feel the vomit creeping up my throat. I screamed again into the darkness. Smash. A soldier bashed his rifle against my leg. I howled in anguish as the tears flowed freely down my face, the only part of me truly free. The soldier ripped the headphones from my ears to scream at me to be silent. I couldn't obey.

Physically and emotionally drained, I could only whimper and cry as the soldier smashed my other leg to pieces.

Wherever I was going, I was going to die.

The truck ground to a stop and a heavy hand landed on my soldier. A voice in my ear yelled at me to stand.

"I can't," I moaned. "My…. my… legs… broken…" I cried.

A huff of exasperation, and then the sound of a wheelchair trundling towards us.

The sack was wrenched from my head, the light blinding. The cold glare of the floodlights left spots dancing on my eyes… as I began to adjust, I took in my surroundings. Tall, chain link fences stretched for miles, surrounded by barbed wire as far as the eye could see. Thousands of people shuffled around a central concrete area wearily and lifelessly, staring out with the same vacant look that so many have worn for years.

My chair rolled towards the gates. I knew that once I passed this threshold, I wasn't coming back. This wasn't a government safe camp; this was a prison camp.

A tall, grey – haired man walked over, his boots clicking on the cold, metal floor. He grabbed my arm outwards and a searing pain coursed through my body.

The smell of burned flesh filled my nostrils.

I looked down at my arm, bright red and burnt. The words VULCAN 01 were branded into my skin.

Now, I'm nothing more than prisoner of the State.

Chapter 5

Freddie

The cluster of Soulless was gaining on me. In the distance, I saw a discarded gun... I reckoned I'd be able to get to it. This would keep them at bay for a few minutes, buying me precious extra time. I turned towards them, appreciating the power that I held in my hands. Firing indiscriminately, the legion of Soulless approaching me was not slowing. They just took the shots and stumbled forwards relentlessly. I needed to get the head, I realised. Aim. Fire. This time, they began to fall as their heads exploded into a bloody mess. Blood and guts sprayed in every direction as the infected continued to fall.

In the distance, I could see a side door swinging open in the breeze. Turning my back on the Soulless, I ran for the door, hoping that this would be my salvation. Maybe Evie is still here? Somehow, I doubted it.

I stepped inside, slamming the door behind me. A long corridor stretched ahead of me, illuminated by a series of humming, flickering emergency lights. There didn't seem to be power, and all I could hear was a deafening silence. The white walls were peppered with bullets and streaks of dried, dark blood.

Picking my way over rotting corpses, my stomach heaved as the smell hit me. They were all soldiers. Clearly, there had been some sort of fight here. And judging by the bullets everywhere, this was human versus human.

I wandered through to the main atrium, feeling somewhat lost and insignificant amongst this cavernous space. A sign pointed towards a cafeteria, at which point I became acutely aware of just how hungry I was. The battered doors swung open, revealing a vast kitchen.

I wasn't going hungry here!

The next morning, I was abruptly awoken by the distant roar of a truck and the faint pulsing of a fleet of helicopters. I sat up; my body numb from the wooden bench. Had the army arrived to recapture their base?

My questions were soon answered by the rhythmic pounding of military boots hitting the cold steel floor of the main atrium. The oppressive silence was replaced with the hum of generators spluttering into life and the static buzz of radio chatter.

Do I hide? Do I show myself?

Running from the noise, I found a small room along the corridor.

Silently, I closed the door and slumped onto the floor.

I looked around; there was a bed and a freshly ironed military uniform hung in the wardrobe, from whoever was here last.

An idea crossed my mind. It was risky, but it was a way to survive. There was no going back from this – if I was to join them, I'd be reduced to nothing more than an expendable killing machine. But the choice facing me was either that, or die, at the hands of the military or the Soulless.

Hastily, I pulled the uniform over my head. A perfect fit.

It felt right, it felt powerful. I felt powerful. Adrenaline courses through my veins as I sling the rifle over my shoulder, waiting for some soldiers to pass my door so I could slip out and join their ranks. Soon enough, the low murmur of voices and the sound of heavy footsteps filled my ears.

Time to go. Time to start my new life.

I opened the door and peered outside. Several men in uniform were up ahead, laughing and joking as they searched for the Soulless or survivors.

"Yo, Jonny, look what I've got here!" One of the soldiers dragged a mutilated Soulless out of a dark corner.

"Watch this," he laughed.

He pulled down his trousers and urinated over the

Soulless, who was trapped under his boot.

The other soldier, Johnny, gave a half-hearted, insincere laugh and turned away.

I could only watch, feeling sick to the stomach, as he smashed their head to pieces.

I decided to follow them, keeping my distance. As I walked, disgusted with what I had just seen, I watched as the same soldier brutally disposed of any infected individuals he came across.

Eventually, they made their way to the cafeteria I slept in last night. The smell of fresh food filled the air, and a lively chatter brought the room back to life.

I joined the back of the queue, ready to eat. No one so far had noticed me; there were so many of them here and all of them a similar age to me – had they been conscripted? Needless to say, I blended in perfectly.

A lump of cold, grey mashed potato landed on my tray, followed by a measly helping of slimy mixed vegetables.

In my past life, there's no way I would've eaten this. But now, to me, this was a feast fit for a king.

I had to try my hardest to fight off my animalistic instinct to devour the plate all at once. These guys have been fed by the military since the start of this thing, I can't stand out by eating like a starved animal.

I savoured every mouthful, the cold potato a liquid gold in my mouth.

A voice echoed over the loudspeaker system, instructing all soldiers to make their way to the main atrium to be addressed by the General.

Not wanting to waste the rest of my food, I quickly finished my meal and followed everyone else outside as the scraping of metal on metal replaced the musical clinking of cutlery on china.

I followed the lead of the soldiers around me, standing to attention for the General. A deathly silence filled the room once more – this man was clearly one that people respected. Or feared.

General Greenfields marched towards the edge of the balcony and began to address his men.

"Good afternoon, gentlemen. I trust that you've all been well fed and watered by our catering staff. Now the real work begins. I have an assignment from the very top of the British Government for a number of you. They need our men to assist in the running and administration of the Vulcan Camp network."

I had no idea what he was talking about.

"Of course, officially these camps do not exist. Hell, I'm

not even supposed to tell you this. But out there... there's nothing left. There's no one for you to tell. I'm not sure that any of those brain dead freaks out there are going to care, huh?"

This earned him a smattering of laughter from the crowd.

"I might as well be honest with you. This job is only for those with the strongest stomachs. No time for messing around here."

I glanced at the guy I saw in the corridor earlier, Johnny's mate. A smirk had crept across his face.

"Anyone that wishes to go to the Vulcan Camps, sign up at the desk by the end of the afternoon. You leave tomorrow, so be ready." He saluted to the crowd and faded back into the shadows.

A long line had already formed with people waiting to sign up to go to the camps.

Why not, I thought. I joined the back of the queue, ready to go.

Someone tapped my shoulder.

"Haven't seen you round here before. You new?"

I turned around cautiously.

"Yeah. You?"

"Yeah. The name's Charlie, Charlie Buckwheat."

"Freddie. You going to the camp?" I relaxed; this guy seemed friendly.

"Yes. I've heard the rumours, but I wanted to see them for myself. I've heard... terrible things about these places. But I can't say anything, you speak out against these guys and you end up like one of those freaks outside." He turned away, realising that he'd said too much.

"I've never heard of them before,' I said. It's true, I had no idea what was going on. And to be honest, I didn't want to know. All I knew was that this was how I was going to get out of here and survive.

We had reached the front of the queue. I stared at the paper, unsure of what name to put down.

Hastily, I scribbled 'Freddie' onto the sheet and turned away, eager to get away from Charlie and his crazy conspiracies.

Wandering without purpose, the prisoners made their way up and down the vast expanse of concrete. These people looked dead, they looked like the Infected that roamed free outside these fences. The ever – present whine of the electric fences filled the air, infiltrating your thoughts and driving you mad.

Someone would bend over, vomiting everywhere. The soldiers look on, laughing. No one cleans it up.

Everyone is coughing, everyone is sneezing.

And still, the world sleeps.

Evie

I walked for what felt like days. I walked on and on, my legs numb and unfeeling. Thirst crept up my throat as I began to run out of water. Unarmed and defenceless, I felt an inch away from death.

An abandoned car sat up ahead on the motorway. The doors were wide open; it was empty. I walked towards it, hoping that it would still work, despite the dents and gashes in the sides.

Sure enough, the keys sat in the ignition, swaying slightly in the gentle breeze. I climbed into the seat, sighing as I sat down. Turning the key, the engine spluttered into life, clouds of smoke oozing from the exhaust. The road ahead was deserted and silent; I slammed my foot on the accelerator and the car lurched forwards.

Once I worked out how to drive consistently, I had the most fun I'd had in weeks. The cool evening breeze danced through my hair as I sped down the motorway, the glittering sunlight bouncing off the windshield. I felt alive, more alive than I had done in forever.

I decided I would just stay on the motorway until I reached the end. Without any direction or plan, I figured that leaving things to chance would be the best option.

Bullet-ridden signs told me that I was heading for London. Nothing could've prepared me for the devastation I was about to witness.

The approach into London, as a child, was always a wondrous occasion. Staring up at the lights and colours of the grand skyscrapers, drinking in the sights and shapes of the city.

But now that was all gone. Everything around the outer circle of the city had been obliterated, a charred stain on the land the only reminder of the past. Sections of chain-link fencing flapped uselessly in the wind; the city had long succumbed to the virus. I drove through what seemed to be an overrun military blockade – the motorway was the only infrastructure not entirely destroyed.

A tattered Change Britain poster fluttered in the wind, Charlie McIntosh's face blackened with soot and grime. The burnt-out husks of skyscrapers and office buildings left an acrid musk over the bleak landscape.

At some point, the sun had retreated behind its grey blanket, leaving a sudden chill in the air. I shivered, although I think more at the horrific sights in front of me than the weather.

The oppressive silence hit me first when I found myself in central London. A once bustling city full of constant noise – now silent.

The only sound for miles around was the chirping of the birds and the occasional buzz of a cricket.

But the roar of the trains and traffic was gone. The whine of the electric pylons absent. Just still and quiet.

I pulled up outside a service station in search of petrol and more importantly, food. It had been hours since I'd last eaten and my supplies were dwindling fast.
Realising that there could be could still be Infected lurking inside the shop, I rummaged through the boot of the car to find something to defend myself with.
All I could find was a rusty tennis bat and a half-dead torch.
I walked up to the door, tennis bat in hand, ready to attack anything that moved. Tapping it with my foot, the door swung open with little resistance. Flicking the torch on, I scanned the room for any sign of life.
Nothing. I sighed, somewhat relaxed. Looking around, the shelves were laden with crisps and chocolate bars, as well as crates of plastic bottles. Just as if I was going shopping on a normal Saturday morning, I began to fill my basket with all the food I could fit inside.
I was about to leave when I spotted something on the very top shelf. A full crate of my favourite chocolates.
I thought, perhaps naively, that I'd be able to reach

them without any great difficulty. All I had to do was climb the shelves. I had just about managed to reach the top when my foot slipped and shot backwards.

The next few seconds seemed to span a lifetime. With an almighty crash, the shelves collapsed on top of me, burying me under a mountain of metal. I could feel the faint trickle of blood cutting tracks through the layers of grime on my forehead.

My ears were ringing from the ear-splitting noise of the fallen shelves, but I was acutely aware of a faint snarling in the distance. Infected. The shop wasn't empty after all. I could see my tennis bat in the distance, but my arms flailed uselessly as I tried to reach for it. The snarling was getting louder. I had to move. Sweat was pouring down my forehead as I began to accept my impending demise.

I pushed upwards with all my strength, determined to move the shelves. They shifted slightly, but still not enough. The unmistakable stench of rotting flesh was beginning to tickle my nostrils... an Infected was getting closer.

Its feet scraped across the tiled floor, a jagged whisper in the gloom. I turned my head to the side, gazing directly into its bloodshot eyes.

I hadn't seen one this close up in a while. My stomach

turned as my eyes passed over its naked stomach; guts and intestines spilled out in every direction. Its skin flapped uselessly as it stumbled towards me. I heaved again as my eyes rested on his face. The skin was charred and burnt, his mouth torn and his jaw limp, as if added by afterthought.

In that second, despite its mindless capacity to gorge on my flesh, I felt a sense of pity for this poor creature. This was somebody's child, somebody's parent. They once had a life, a purpose.

Shaking these thoughts, terror coursed through my veins as the Infected drew closer. I could hear its rasping breath cut through the silence. Shuffle. Snarl. Growl. The creature was standing directly above me. Drip. A single drop of saliva landed on my forehead, trickling into my hair.

I could feel its breath on my cheeks. Bloodshot eyes staring into mine. On its knees. Face, closer, almost touching mine. Teeth snapping.

This is it. Breathe. In. Out.

And just as I thought it was all over, its body slackened. It toppled backwards, crashing onto the floor with a dull thud. Adrenaline still coursing through my veins, I sighed with relief.

I looked up and jumped as I stared at the legs of my

apparent saviour. She spoke, her voice filling the room. "You bitten?"

"No. Thanks to you." I replied cautiously; I had no idea who this girl was.

"My pleasure." She twirled her bow in her hand as she spoke.

"You're hurt," she said, gesturing to the gash on my forehead. Realising that I was still trapped under the metal shelving, she lifted them away.

I tried to stand up and winced as I put pressure on my foot. Looking down at my legs, I grimaced as I took stock of the extent of my injuries. I was a bloody mess of cuts and bruises, and my ankle looked pretty broken to me.

My saviour was still standing by the door.

"Come with me," she said. "We have a safe compound, a doctor to treat you. You will be safe with us." Smiling, she looked to me for a response.

"I'm Abi; you can trust me."

My mind was racing. She seemed nice, but can you really trust anyone out here? For all I knew, she just wanted my food. After all, everyone has to survive.

But I couldn't even stand up properly, let alone defend myself out there. Either way, things were looking pretty grim for me.

"Okay. Let's go," I said.

I really hoped I was making the right decision.

She put her arm around me, and together we hobbled towards her car. My trolley of goods sat abandoned behind us.

I lay down across the back seat of the car, hoping that sleep would soon take me. Abi jumped into the front and the engine rumbled into life... then darkness.

We were running, screaming. These monsters chasing us from behind, shredding anyone that came near. And then they would stand again, join these killing machines in their crusade against us. My friends, running at us, trying to kill us. Snarl. Blood. Flesh. Bone. Explosion.

I woke up with a start, sweat pouring down my forehead. Since that day in the school, I haven't been able to close my eyes without the horror and trauma flooding back.

I suddenly realised that the car had stopped, and Abi was staring at me. Looking out of the window, all I could see were fields for miles around.

'Well, this is how it all ends,' I thought, 'Dead in a ditch.'

"You alright?" she asked, her voice softer than earlier. "You screamed."

I felt my cheeks flame with embarrassment. Perhaps she wasn't about to kill me after all.

"N...Nightmares. Can't sleep," I stammered. I felt so stupid right now.

"Hey, no need to be ashamed," she whispered. "We've all been through hell these past couple of months."

She wasn't wrong.

The first thing that hits you is the smell. Some of the huts are worse than others, but this one was particularly bad. Pools of vomit lay on the floor. The thick stench of stale urine hung low, and the overpowering stink of body odour hits like a punch to the gut. But above all of this, stronger than everything else, was an overwhelming air of pure sadness and desperation. People sat, stripped of their humanity, wallowing in their own filth and misery.

Chapter 6

Freddie

I woke up, staring at the flickering fluorescent light above me. I already felt the dull ache of a trapped nerve.

My new uniform lay draped on the back of my chair. Today was the day we moved – the trucks were coming to take us to the camps later that morning. It felt as though a new chapter in my life was dawning, as if I was rewriting my story. For the first time since the world went to pieces, I felt as though I had a purpose. I felt like I belonged.

Meandering over to the shower, I rested my head against the cool glass as the warm water washed over me. The steam swirled around the bathroom, twisting into faces and shadows. I thought of Evie, wondered if she was still alive. Wondered if I would ever see her again. And my mum… thinking of her was too painful.

I stepped out of the shower, drying myself and cleaning my teeth. The uniform sat on its chair, beckoning me towards it with some magical compulsion.

'Vulcan.' Just the name sounded powerful, menacing.

It was a perfect fit... it just felt so right. As if this was something I was always meant to do.

I headed towards the cafeteria, nodding to my fellow comrades in their new uniform. As we entered, the soldiers eating gave us a rousing cheer, applauding us as we walked inside.

"You're doing God's work!" one man shouted.

I felt a warm glow inside, this was all the validation I needed. My fellow Vulcan soldiers stood beside me, grinning at the crowd of cheering soldiers.

We sat down at a table reserved just for us, as if we were royalty. Breakfast came to us this morning, an extra helping of their trademark watery porridge. No use complaining though, food isn't exactly in plentiful supply these days.

"So, Freddie, are you looking forward to this?" I looked up, realising someone was talking to me.

"Uhh... yeah. Should be interesting," I smiled. If I was being honest, I wasn't exactly sure what to expect. I heard someone say that they were the Government safe camps, but deep down, I had my doubts.

The rest of the morning passed by in something of a blur. I remember sitting outside on the brick wall feeling the cold wind against my cheeks, the rain soaking through my hair. It made me feel alive.

12:30. The Vulcan soldiers were ordered into the main atrium. I watched as the giant steel gates rolled open, flooding the building with natural light. The rest of the soldiers stood round the balcony above us, cheering and clapping as we headed out towards the grey trucks.

I sat down on one of the benches and sighed as Charlie sat down next to me. Not prepared to spend the next couple of hours listening to his crazy theories about where we were going, I fished my phone from my pocket. I felt like I was holding a priceless treasure – some of the other soldiers looked up in amazement as the cool glow of the screen lit up my face.

It was by some miracle that I had found a charger and a pair of headphones in the room I stayed in back at the military compound; I sat back and let the music wash over me.

A few minutes later, the engine spluttered into life and I felt the truck pull away.

As we bounced over the craters and holes in the plaza, I couldn't help but wonder what was in store for us.

I remembered listening to these songs with Evie on hazy summer afternoons in times gone by –

the bleak winter approaching couldn't feel further from those days.

Life was just so simple then.

I must've fallen asleep at some point along the way. Charlie prodded my arm, whispering that we had arrived. The back doors swung open, flooding the truck with light. I stumbled out, blinking as the sun hit my eyes.

We all stood, staring with disbelief at the sight ahead of us. Miles and miles of barbed wire and metal fencing. Vast expanses of concrete. Rows and rows of temporary buildings.

A small, grey haired man was walking towards us, clutching a stack of ID tags. He was wearing a similar uniform to us, rifle slung over his shoulder.

"You must be the new recruits, right?" He spoke with a thick Northern accent – I didn't realise just how far we had travelled.

We all nodded and turned to follow him back down the hill.

He ushered us through the wrought - iron gates, and directed us to a small, inconspicuous building on the edge of the compound, and into a surprisingly comfortable room.

Taking our seats around an oak table, we looked towards the screen at the end of the room.

The words VULCAN ONE were emblazoned on the screen in bright red lettering. Just that in itself looked threatening, given the context of our surroundings. A stack of papers landed in front of each of us. The words 'SENSITIVE – OFFICIAL DOCUMENTS' stared back up at me.

I doubted that whatever was inside was going to make for particularly pleasant reading.

Skimming through the papers, I felt sickened at the regime I had just joined. If I could see Charlie's face right now, I'm sure he'd have a smug "I told you so" plastered across it.

Then I noticed a detail that shocked me to my core. This place has been operating for the last 6 years. Six years... that means that since I was 10 years old, this regime has been routinely murdering people. Locking them up. Leaving them to die.

And suddenly it all made sense. All those people that simply vanished. My primary school teacher.

My friend, Josh, who campaigned against Change Britain. Evie's dad?

They all came to these places. They came here to die.

They came here to die at the hands of people like me.

I felt sick.

The short, grey haired man reappeared.

"I hope those documents provided some context as to the scale and nature of the operation here." He paused, sucking the air between his teeth.

"Your job here is very simple. Maintain order, punish those that break the rules and never, ever talk to the inmates. And keep your mask on at all times, they must never see your full face. Is that clear?" We all nodded in understanding.

One of his assistants swept up the documents and tossed them into a shredder. With a mechanical hiss, it chewed them up effortlessly, removing any trace of the evil forces at work. I stood up, my mind reeling from what I had just learned.

We were led to our accommodation, flanked by a legion of seasoned Vulcan guards. The inmates scurried in all directions as we approached, their torn, grimy clothes billowing in the wind.

As the breeze caught their clothes, I couldn't help but notice the brands that each of them wore on their arms. The words 'VULCAN ONE' stamped into their flesh.

Prisoners of the State.

---

*It's now 2029. The camps have been operating for six years.
Until the Outbreak, they were doing their job. The
population was shrinking. Like a well-oiled machine, new
inmates arrived and the old purged. With nearly every
outspoken opposition to the government silenced and locked
away in the Vulcan Camps, the authoritarian grip of the
government was only getting stronger by the day.
Everybody conformed to the ideology of Charlie McIntosh,
everyone obeyed without question.*

*But when Virus Z-19 ravaged the land, these camps that
once contained the scourges of society suddenly became the
last outposts of civilization. The last safe locations in
Britain. The irony in that was too much to bear.*

Evie

Abi turned around in her seat, proudly declaring that we had arrived. I sat up, wincing and rubbing my eyes as the events of the past few hours came flooding back. Looking out of the window, I couldn't help but feel a little underwhelmed as my eyes rested on abandoned warehouse. The rust–red bricks were carpeted in moss and ivy, the windows smashed and boarded up. A steady stream of water poured from the roof as the guttering had seemingly long collapsed. Weeds pushed up through the cracks of the surrounding plaza.

But then there was this unique hive of activity. People were hard at work planting seeds to harvest and chopping up wood to carve into furniture. In the distance, I could see a small infirmary.

Two men, perhaps in their forties, came running over to the truck. They hugged Abi, who I later discovered was their sister, and returned with a stretcher.

People stopped and stared as they carted me across the compound towards the infirmary. My cheeks singed with embarrassment as I realised just how weak I looked.

Hopefully Abi would keep the true story of how she

found me to herself.

The doctor was a kindly old man that went by the name of Geoff. He bandaged my ankle; it was broken - and treated my many cuts and scrapes. I'll never forget how odd the whole ordeal felt; society had collapsed outside and yet this guy was pulling on rubber gloves and treating me as if we were in a professional hospital. He left me to rest, telling me that someone would come to see me in the morning.

For the first time since we left the military base at the start of the outbreak, I had a proper bed again. Maybe staying here wouldn't be such a bad idea.

Hours passed, but still sleep wouldn't take me. Rain lashed against the windows as the wind screeched through the gaps under the door. The occasional flash of lighting illuminated the room a brilliant white every time I began to drift off.

Running. I'm always running. The heavy, laboured footsteps of the Infected are getting closer. My heels pound the soil, kicking clouds of dust behind me. Blood… I can smell blood. I look up. Dead animals hang from the trees, their blood dripping, pouring, gushing. The Infected stop, their hands clawing upwards, desperate for a taste. Blood, everywhere. All I see is red. I turn, desperate for a way out of this nightmare. The trees are getting smaller,

113

I can feel it. Or am I getting bigger? Suffocating. Can't breathe. Blood. Drip, drip, drip. Warm blood, fresh blood. Drip, Drip, Drip. The bodies sway in the wind. I look up again. Humans. I see Freddie. I see my mum. I see myself. Drip. Drip. Drip. Blood. All I see is red. All I see is red.

Drip. Drip. Drip. Sunshine floods through the window as the rain from the storm of last night falls away. The rhythmic splash brings me back to reality as the horrors of my nightmares began to fade away.

Dr. Geoff walked in, clipboard in hand. He asked me how I was feeling, and then told me that he was able to discharge me into the community.

Abi walked in, pushing a wheelchair. She smiled tiredly and helped me into the seat.

Part of me felt that singe of embarrassment across my cheeks again. What use would a girl in a wheelchair be to these people? They want to survive, not look after an extra burden.

But perhaps I was wrong. As we made our way across the compound, members of the community came and said hello, presenting me with food and flowers, wishing me a speedy recovery. Everyone was so friendly... it felt like being welcomed into a family.

"Welcome to Creek Hills. You must be Evie?" He smiled through his glasses, the corners of his eyes creasing.

"My name is Kieran. I'm the Chief, and I'm going to look after you," he said.

We walked back round to the main compound and he talked animatedly, describing in detail their defence systems and how they feed their people.

But I wasn't really listening to what he was saying. His words faded out, replaced with a shrill ringing sound. Shapes twisted and contorted in front of my eyes... I was falling, I was back in that forest.

Drip. Drip. Drip. Blood, blood, more blood. I look to the sky, past the hanging bodies, and all I see is a vast expanse of red. A whispering, a chanting, a rhythmic beat of a drum. Closer, closer. A step forward. Blood bubbles underfoot. The chanting is getting closer. The drums getting louder. The blood dripping faster, always there, drip, drip, drip. I feel sick, I feel trapped.

I can feel my mind collapsing. An explosion rocks the forest. Mud and rocks fly upwards. Blood shoots from the ground, spraying in every direction. I look around. The ground is imploding, the same fountains in every direction. I look to the ground. I stand alone on an island. And then I'm falling, I'm falling down to into Hell.

"Quick, get her some water. And find some blankets, she's shivering." Someone called faintly in the distance. I opened my eyes, blinking as the bright sunlight fills my eyes once more. Dr Geoff was running towards me. Was I sick?

Every time I closed my eyes, the trauma comes back. The blood, the faces, the cries of those I couldn't save.

The Chief wheeled me through to the main compound, insisting that I eat something. We reached the kitchen, the unmistakable aroma of fresh vegetable soup taking me back to my childhood.

My grandad always used to make his 'special recipe' when we came to visit, it was truly something special.

He returned minutes later clutching two bowls of hot, steaming soup. Setting them down on the table with a dull thud, he pushed one in my direction.

I twirled my spoon around the soup, tracing patterns in the surface, watching them fade away into the bowl.

"You have a home here," Kieran whispered.

Chapter 7

Freddie

My alarm rung out into the darkness. God, I hated the night patrol. I stared up at the ceiling, questioning how exactly I got here. Until a few months ago, I was just a normal teenager. Now I'm a murderer. I glanced at my watch. Time to go; if I'm late again I'll end up stuck on the night shift for the rest of the week.

I picked my gun up and flicked my torch on. The door swung open with a creak, prompting grunts from the other sleeping soldiers.

I looked to the heavens, the moon shining bright overhead, the one constant in this broken world. An owl screeched in the distance, echoing through the darkness. I couldn't help but feel slightly uneasy out here alone; the night-time was oppressive, crushing.

The gravel crunched underfoot, every step echoing across the complex.

I felt nothing as I shone my torches into each hut, taking a cursory glance into the squalor and filth, moving on before I properly looked.

It was just before dawn when I spotted the drone. At first, I didn't even recognise what I was seeing.

I stood staring at the sky as I tried to work out what it was. And then I realised – it was filming. Someone out there knew what was going on here.

I didn't know what to do. It was too late; as I fumbled through my pockets to find my radio, it had already melted back into the gloom.

I carried on walking until dawn raised her sombre grey army; rain clouds gathered threateningly overhead. The bell rang out into the silence, stirring the inmates from their rest. I climbed a watchtower, leaning out into the rain as I watched them file out of their cabins, one by one. They looked empty, broken, soulless. Reduced to something less than human.

Unfazed by the pouring rain, they trudged out into the storm. My knuckles were going white as I gripped the railings; every day here, I felt a little less human.

I heard a shout in the distance. People were shouting; a woman was screaming. A mother emerged from one of the huts, clutching something wrapped in a bundle of blankets. And then I realised – it was her baby. Her baby was dead.

I watched as she sunk to her knees, screaming, shaking her fists at the sky. Soldiers were running over, keen to quell the unrest.

She saw them coming and rose to her feet. Still screaming, she ran at them, hurling handfuls of stones and gravel at their faces. The soldiers grabbed her, asked her to calm down.

Further enraged by this statement, she kept screaming and kicking. The soldiers looked at each other. One of them stepped back. Raised his gun. Shot her.

She fell backwards, landing next to her dead son. Blood pooled around her head.

And still, I felt nothing.

Evie

A few weeks had passed, and I was beginning to feel like myself again. My ankle had healed; I was out of my chair, but my body was still littered with scars and bruises.

Life at Creek Hills was simple, but good. And the awe and magnitude of the operation here was never lost on me, not even for a second.

Kieran put me to work once I was feeling better; everyone here has a job to do. I spend my time outside, planting seeds and picking vegetables. The fresh air gives me a sense of freedom, a sense of peace.

But one thing hasn't changed. The nightmares, the nightmares won't leave me. Every time I close my eyes, the same horrors come back, the blood, the forest, the bodies in the trees.

The bell tolls in the distance, calling us in for dinner. As we all take our seats, a warm and jovial conversation fills the room.

But a respectful hush fell when Kieran stood up on the balcony and began to talk, his nightly speeches something of a tradition around here.

"Ladies and gentlemen. Tonight, my lecture will be short, but sad. For years, I have had my suspicions about this, but last night I got all the proof I needed. Let me ask you something. Over the past six years, how many of you knew someone that just simply... vanished?"

This prompted a murmur across the room. And then I thought back to last year, to my dad. How he just disappeared. How the police wanted nothing to do with it.

I sat up, suddenly intrigued.

"I take it that many of you know what I'm talking about. For the last six years, the government has been carrying out a political cleansing under our noses." He began to shout, his voice trembling with passion.

"Your government, Charlie McIntosh, Change Britain and those BioFlex... monsters, have been killing our families. Killing our friends."

The room darkened as a projector flickered into life. An audible gasp swept across the room.

His video showed miles and miles of barbed wire and metal fencing enclosing hundreds of huts and buildings. I could see soldiers patrolling with their guns, searchlights sweeping across the complex.

"We have the weapons and the resources to free them. Tomorrow, we go to war against the Government. Tomorrow, we go to fight for everyone that has disappeared." He shouted those last words, stepping down from the stage to raucous applause. People stood on the tables, shouting and cheering, a blend of fury and fierce determination, and admiration for their leader.

That night, I couldn't sleep. I tossed and turned on my small bed, thinking about what the next day held. What if Freddie had ended up in one of these places? What if he was a prisoner there? I was determined to go and fight.

What if this is where my dad went?

I'm drowning, I can't breathe. I claw my way upwards, only to get dragged back down again. Hands close around my ankles, pulling me. I open my eyes. Blood. I blink. I'm back in the forest. I'm going insane, I'm losing my mind, I can feel it. Voices whisper in the back of my head. Everywhere, voices, crying, shouting, screaming. A wind blows. The leaves are falling off the trees, red and cold. The sky is darkening, the moon covering the sun. An eclipse, maybe. The wind is getting stronger. Birds screeching. Dogs barking. Children crying. And then darkness. Silence. Nothing. A cold hand strokes my face. Death himself stares me in the eye. "Come with me, Evie," he whispers. "Come to me."

I woke with a start, panting and shaking. The girl in the bed next to me stared at me, a look of concern plastered across her face.

Before she said anything, I stood up and smiled tiredly after I told her that I was fine.

I got dressed and headed downstairs, joining the sizeable crowd waiting to listen to the Chief speak.

I was blown away at just how ready the people here were to lay down their lives just on the words of their leader.

But, I suppose, that's what people have been doing for the last decade.

Kieran stood on the balcony of the warehouse and addressed us all before we headed out. He told us that history would remember us as heroes, as the ones who finally revealed the treachery and corruption at the heart of the British institution. Expose BioFlex as the evil monsters they are and restore order to this broken world.

He spoke of how freeing those locked up today will lay the foundations for a new civilization tomorrow. I felt pride and determination swell across my chest as his words washed over us, goose bumps creeping across my skin as I thought of the task ahead of us today. A galvanising cheer went up from the listening crowd, and we surged towards the doors.

We filed onto the trucks, and as the engines roared into life, I thought back to the last time I was sat on a truck like this. Less than a month ago, yet it felt like a lifetime ago. The fear I felt then is a distant memory now. And yet, there's still an element of the unknown here – I have no idea where I am headed.

For all I know, I'm being driven towards my death.

The fields flash by in bursts of green and colour, a stark contrast to the grey concrete of the burnt-out towns and homes. The faces of those from my old life pass across my mind, my mum, my friends… Freddie.

I know I'll never see him again. He's probably dead… I just hope he didn't turn. I hope, wherever he is, he's resting in peace.

I close my eyes, hoping that sleep will take me.

'Come to me, Evie. Come to me.' An ethereal voice in the distance. I walk towards it, intrigued. I get to the edge of the forest, the same forest I always end up in. I try to turn around, I know what's coming. But I'm pushing back against a tidal wave, an invisible force. The sky darkens, blood red once more. Thunder cracks. Lightning splits the sky in two. And then the heavens open, but it isn't rain, it never is. Blood pours down on me, cleansing me of my sins.

And the faces, the faces, the faces… the faces, they all whisper to me. My head fills with the whispers, the cries, the moans, the screams, I can't take it, I can't take it. But it's no use, I'm trapped. I run, tears pouring down my face. But they're not my tears, it's the blood of Everest, the blood of all those children that I killed, the blood of all those children I left to die. The blood of all those Infected that I killed to let me live. The blood of my guilt, the blood of my survival. I reach a bridge. A river runs below. The sun shines. Water flows. I jump.

I wake with a start as a voice at the front of the truck tells us to get ready, we're almost there. I check my gun; the chamber is full of bullets. My knives are ready in their sheaths and the bullet proof vest tightened. I looked around the truck and the faces staring back at me – gaunt, hollow and scared. But within each of them, a fierce determination set in their eyes, ready to be on the right side of history.

The truck pulled to a stop, and someone unbolted the doors. We jumped out and assembled ourselves into our factions, ready to fight. Kieran addressed us again, telling us that we are strong enough to take on the military.

Somehow, deep down, I doubted that. But I kept my doubts to myself.

I could see the camp in the distance, the miles of barbed wire and metal fencing. It was certainly an imposing sight. We began to march forwards, through an abandoned industrial estate. The rusted metal shutters whistling in the wind, a relic of a different world. I felt a desperate sadness knowing that whatever happened today, the world would never be restored to the previous order.

But then again, our world has been broken for a very long time. Longer than this virus, longer than my lifetime.

A girl next to me grabbed my hand. "I don't want to do this, I can't even fire a gun," she whispered.

I tried my best to reassure her, despite sharing her same qualms about this operation.

We had arrived. Time to light things up.

At some point, our ragtag militia had managed to acquire some military grade rockets. Nobody had known what to do with them at the time, but in his wisdom, Kieran had saved them for a rainy day.

Today was that rainy day. They positioned them towards the front of the gates and got ready to fire. I crouched to the ground, bracing myself for the explosion.

A blinding flash, followed by a deafening crash, blew the entrance wide open. A rousing cheer went up from the militia – secrecy was not really a problem now.

We walked forwards, each of us firing a shot into the air. Sirens began to wail, and soldiers came pouring out of every building. Those being held ran out too – I saw a girl struggling in a wheelchair in the distance. I broke away from the group and ran over to help her – she wasn't going to get out with the rest if someone didn't help her. Kieran was shouting to the residents of the camp to run for the exit – and they did, in their thousands.

I reached the girl in the wheelchair, realising that both of her legs had been broken.

"Did they do this to you?" I asked as I pushed her towards the exit.

"Yes. They hurt everyone. Every morning, they take two or three people from each unit and they never come back."

So, this really was a death camp.

We were doing pretty well; we had almost reached the entrance when a masked soldier stepped into our way. Without a second thought, he fired at the girl in the wheelchair. Her chest was ripped apart, her torn clothes stained with spasms of dark red.

"What do we have here then, huh?" He spoke with a familiar voice, he sounded like someone from long ago. Or my fear – ridden brain was playing tricks.

He spoke again. "Some sort of vigilante? You should've known better than to mess with BioFlex and the Government, this will only get you killed. And today, you're going to die."

No, I definitely recognised his voice. Something in the way he was standing, the set of his shoulders, how his hands were clasped behind him... it was painfully familiar.

I caught a glimpse of his face. I stumbled to my knees.

Drip, drip, drip

The world around me went silent.

I was back in the forest, the skies blood red.

I felt sick.

The trees closed in, the ivy winding around my legs.

A blow to the stomach.

I couldn't move, I couldn't run this time.

For the first time in weeks, tears flowed freely down my cheeks.

My head snaps upwards, unable to stop the screams.

My world, my best friend, standing right in front of me.

The blood red rain washes over me, staining me.

With a gun to my head.

I see my body hanging again, swaying in the wind.

"Freddie?" I snivelled.

Freddie

The sirens echoed eerily across the compound, waking me from my sleep. I've never heard these before... something bad must be happening. One of the officers shouted something about a vigilante attack... I groaned as I got out of bed. Hastily, I shoved on my uniform and my mask, and got ready to fight. I knew that whatever was unfolding outside would be bad, and we were all expected to fight.

Boom. A deafening explosion rocked the building. Chunks of the ceiling collapsed, and a thick layer of dust settled over everything. I choked and pulled on a mask. That was the number one rule here – never let them see your face.
I wonder what Evie would think if she saw me here. What would she say? What would she think of me now, the monster that I have become?

I ran outside and surveyed the carnage. The gates had been blown wide open and some nutter with a megaphone was yelling at the inmates to run for it.
I watched as my fellow soldiers surrounded him. I watched as he dropped the megaphone to the ground. I watched as they killed him.

I watched and didn't feel at all.

I could see the girl in the wheelchair in the distance. Rachael, I think her name is – I took her to the medic when her legs were smashed up. Some vigilante type was pushing her chair towards the exit, talking as they went. I knew I had to stop them, no one was allowed to leave. They were headed right for me.

This was going to be fun. I stepped into their path, sensing the fear on their faces. Rachael was quivering in her chair, weak and feeble. My cold, uncaring hand pulled the trigger, snatching her life with the crack of a bullet.

The vigilante had dropped to her knees, crying. I guess she knew she was going to be next. I stood over her, powerful. Adrenaline coursing through my veins, I knew I had to kill her.

No, I wanted to kill her. A thirst for blood had seemingly overtaken me. I wanted to be violent. I wanted to kill.

I raised my gun up to her head.

Pressed the cold barrel to her skin. Saw the desperate look in her eyes.

She whispered a word. I didn't hear, and to be honest, I didn't care. I couldn't see her face properly through the mask, but I knew she was still crying.

Crack.

Her body fell backwards, lifeless and still. Blood trickled out of her forehead.

But something didn't feel right. A terrible guilt crept over my body, prickling the back of my mind, thorny and sharp. I took off my mask.

I looked at her body. Looked at her face.
Looked at Evie.

An animalistic howl escaped from deep within my soul. I sank to my knees, the emotional anguish a physical torment. I screamed as the world burned around me, as my life came crashing down.
I killed my best friend. My best friend that I've known since I was born. The friend I have shared everything with. The friend that used to joke with me on the way to school, the friend that used to tease me in class.
Now dead, by my own hand.

I sat next to her body for what felt like hours. Bullets flew overhead and screams echoed around me. My tears mixed with the pools of her blood. I couldn't think of anything but Evie, of what I had done.
I looked up at last and found the place deserted. Dead

bodies lay lifeless across the compound, but both soldiers and inmates alike had disappeared.

I picked up her body and began to walk.

Later that evening, I set up camp on a bridge over the river. I pulled out my journal, as I did every evening, and began to write.

But I'm distracting myself. Just writing down my experiences, my life, just to blank out what I've done. Because the guilt of this will eat me away forever. I killed Evie. Every time I close my eyes, every time I think of my past, I see her, dead. Dead on the floor because of the monster I have become. Dead because I chose power, corruption and safety over decency and morals. I should've left when I had the chance, that first day when the military arrived. Or I should've let them kill me. Either way, I shouldn't be here now. I shouldn't be standing here alive, when Evie is dead.

I closed the journal and set it down in my bag. I knew I had one thing left to do.

I hauled Evie's body down towards the riverbank and lay her down. I couldn't dig, but I sat through the night carving a headstone with a piece of wood and my knife. As the first rays of dawn began to peek through the clouds, I placed the wooden piece into the ground.

I walked back up to the bridge and watched the sun rise. Dawn gave way to grey, and the grey gave way to rain. I stood, feeling the cold water wash over my body and peck at my face.

I could not go on any longer.

There is no more civilization. There is no more hope. And for me, there is no salvation. I died when I shot Evie.

And now my soul must join hers.

I stepped up onto the railing, embracing the growing storm. I stared out into the cold, unforgiving world. I stared and thought about all I had done. All those I had killed. I thought of my friends. I thought of my mother… oh my mother… what would she make of her son now?

A steely resolve pushed these thoughts from my mind. There was just one thing to do now.

I stepped forwards.

With that step, I instantly found peace. My body absolved of all guilt; my mind free again. The rain cleared; the sun shone. I saw Evie's face again, saw her smile twisting in the water. Saw her hand reach up from the bottom of the river, clasping mine. Heard the words,

"I forgive you."

A cold wind blew through the empty huts. The only sound – the faint snarling of the Infected in the distance. The flickering searchlights illuminate the burnt – out ruins of Camp Vulcan. Bodies, lifeless and bloody, litter the compound as the vast iron gates swing limply in the wind. Fascism has finally fallen, but here, there are no winners. And still, the world burns.

Epilogue

Part One

Jonathon Percival sat in a cold, dark bunker alongside the Prime Minister. Neither said a word, neither spoke. But there was a palpable tension in the air, almost thick enough to touch. Their eyes were fixated on the TV screen ahead of them, watching a replay of the collapse of one of the Vulcan Camps. The camp liberated by 'vigilante militia,' was how the military described it.

Turning to Jonathon, the Prime Minister began to speak.

"You've known as long as I have that the Vulcan Camp project was the only way to ensure the future stability of our country. Our population was just too large, we had to do this. You know that, don't you?" The Prime Minister spoke like a broken man, seeking validation in an old friend.

He carried on. "But your virus messed things up for us. We weren't ready for this. It was too soon. And now, this great civilization that I tried to save, you destroyed." He pulled a gun on Jonathon, staring with a cold smile.

Jonathon knew this was going to happen. The Prime Minister was surrounded by BioFlex soldiers. Each of them armed with a gun, trained directly at him.

Aware that this would be the end of him, he stood up and walked to the door.

"Let him go," said Jonathon.

He walked out of the door, and in doing so, made Jonathon Percival, CEO of BioFlex, the most important and powerful man in this broken shell of a country.

Jonathon knew that he couldn't leave the remaining camps to operate as they were, they too would eventually fall just as Vulcan 01. He searched in his desk for a forgotten project, his earliest idea as a junior BioFlex scientist.

Project Hollowgram. A way to cryogenically preserve huge numbers of people in a safe location following the collapse of society, in the eventual hope that they would wake up into a restored world.

Now was the time.

***

Part Two

That last morning in the camp there was an air of excitement about. Ever since they told us last week that we were being transferred, people stopped disappearing in the morning. There seemed to be some hope for our future. We wondered where we were going, if we were being released, if we would see our families again. If we could go home.

Little did we know that the world outside these fences was gone. When the busses drove us out of those gates, we saw a world on fire. Nobody told us what had happened out there. The man in the uniform told us that we were the lucky ones, that we would be safe with them, but I don't believe them.

I've been stuck in this camp for the last five years, since 2024. My life has been a dull monotony of sleep, food, exercise, repeat every single day of the year. No Christmas, no birthday, nothing. Here, you exist simply as a prisoner of the State, no longer a person but an inconvenience, a blot in their grand plan for society. And they tell us nothing of the world outside either; I remember the European War starting the year before I was arrested, but nothing more.

We heard whisperings of a disease, a 'zombie virus',

but no one told us anything more than that.

And we were one of the lucky ones. To survive this long… it was a miracle. Disease would spread like wildfire and we only got one shower a week. There was no medicine, and no doctor if you got sick. If you got ill, you died.

But now, at last, things were looking better. Or at least, I thought they were.

"Aazim, are you coming?" Oliver and Josh stood by the door, bags in hand, ready to leave.

"I want to go back to the Patch one last time," said Josh. The Patch was where they left the ashes of those killed inside the camps. His girlfriend, Ava, was murdered last year.

"I have to say goodbye," he whispered. A singular tear leaked out of the corner of his eye. Since she was killed last year, the three of us have been inseparable. That's how you survive in this place, form a group and stick by them no matter what. Of course, the Uniforms don't care about that. Every morning, they'd choose one or two inmates from each block, and they'd never return. That was the reality of life inside Vulcan.

I walked out of the door, closing it gently behind me. The three of us headed away from the evacuation busses to the other side of the compound, Josh leading the way. Oliver and I hung back, thinking it best to leave him to his grief.

A Uniform crossed our path, rifle swung over his shoulder.

"On the bus, all of you." His thick Northern accent cut across the plaza, cold and menacing.

"Oi, you too. On the bus, now!" Josh ignored him and carried on walking towards the Patch.

The Uniform raised his gun to Josh's head.

"Last chance, son." I think I detected a hint of emotion in his voice. But he has a job to do.

Josh ignored him and carried on walking. He reached the edge of the Patch and sank to his knees. A single tear rolled down his cheek, splashing into the dust.

All this time, the Uniform looked on, torn between duty and humanity.

"Do it," Josh called out with a steely resolve.

"I'm not leaving her."

Crack. The whistle of a bullet. Thud.

His body slumped forwards, blood pooling into the orange dust. One final blood stain on this land.

Oliver and I walked back towards the bus in a stunned silence. Neither of us would ever talk about what we just saw again. We took our seats as the bus roared into life, taking us towards our new futures. None of us were prepared for what we were about to see.

The world we were stolen from years ago was long gone. Dead bodies lay piled up at the sides of the roads. Houses sat, abandoned and burning. Electricity pylons lay on their sides, their cables strangling the trees. Entire towns had been wiped out, the bombed out remains smouldering gently. We drove past checkpoint after checkpoint, each of them destroyed and useless.

What exactly had happened out here?

As we drove into London, the answer became a little clearer. Bodies hung, reminiscent of a public execution, the corpses flailing and snarling.

They looked like zombies.

A shout came from the front of the bus. The Uniform driving cursed, smashing his hand on the horn as the bus screeched to a halt.

Something was wrong. I could hear a low snarling sound through the window. A hand smacked the glass. And another, and another. All around the bus, bloated, rotten hands pounded the glass.

Nervously, I peered outside, unsure of what sights awaited.

A legion of half rotten, snarling, limp – haired monsters.

Cracks were beginning to appear in the glass. The Uniforms hovered anxiously, unsure of what to do. And then the creatures burst through the windscreen.

They poured through the glass, oblivious to the shards slicing them to ribbons, chewing through and biting anyone that got in their way. The Uniform sat in the driver's seat spasmed as they tore through his neck, blood spraying in every direction.

Eager for their next victim, they stumbled down the aisle of the bus, biting and snapping. Children screamed, but they had nowhere to turn. I hid under the seat, trembling with fear.

Uniforms began firing indiscriminately, screaming at us to get hide below the seats. Bullets ricocheted in all directions, my ears ringing from the noise.

A whisper against my skin. I look up. I stare into its eyes, bloodshot and grey. Its teeth are closing in, snapping around my arm. I try and pull back, too late. It has me. I stifle a scream. Teeth sink into flesh. Flesh rips from bone. Blood flows down my arm.

Bang. A Uniform shot it. I pulled my jumper over the

bite, hoping that wherever we were going, they would be able to cure me.

Shaken, the few of us that survived climbed out from our shelter. I looked around; blood splatters covered the walls and dead bodies lay strewn in every direction.

My eyes rested on Oliver.

I felt vomit rise up my throat. Blood pooled around his corpse, his throat torn out and chewed. I couldn't hold it back. As I looked down at his gaping stomach, I gagged, spraying vomit all over his dead body.

The bus finally pulled away after the remaining Uniforms managed to take back control, the bodies rolling across the floor as it turned. I stared out of the cracked, bloody window, trying to take my mind off of what had just happened.

A tattered, grimy Change Britain poster flapped uselessly in the wind as we approached the heart of the government.

Decorations lined the streets in preparation for the anniversary of Independence Day; I remembered the 'celebrations' from before I was locked away. The day of the year where they celebrated Britain's biggest political mistake with more propaganda and more lies.

But now the old order has fallen. And with it, civilization as I knew it.

I rested my head against the cool glass, trying to distract myself from the fever tearing through my body. My head was like a vice. I could hear my blood rush through my ears. Every sound was ten times, a hundred times louder than it should be.

My eyes blurred in and out of focus... something didn't feel right at all. The bus pulled to a stop outside a vast stone building.

The doors opened and a Uniform stepped on board.

"Welcome to BioFlex," he smiled. Something felt wrong, the name sounded familiar.

"If you would all like to follow me, I will take you for your medical examinations."

He stepped off again, wiping his boots on the grass. One by one we rose, making our way towards the door. I stood. My legs shook uncontrollably. Sunlight. Too bright. Blurring again. Can't walk straight. Shapes, colours. The pain. A pulsing sound. Blood rushing through my ears.

A hand on my face. Torch in my eyes. Light, fading. Falling. Darkness. Freedom.

***

Part Three

The rest of the busses pulled up outside the BioFlex compound. A gunshot rang out as an Infected fell to the ground. A steady stream of people, all ages and races, walk towards the gates, lining up to be admitted. The ones that didn't make it through, the ones that were sick, quietly disappeared for the sake of the greater good.

They filed in in their hundreds, each taking a seat in the vast atrium of the BioFlex compound. Humanity reunited at last.

Jonathon walked up to the stage, his footsteps echoing off the cold metal walls. He stood at the lectern, gripping the metal sides till his fingertips went white. Gazing round the room, his ominous presence filled the room with an icy silence.

"I must say, I'm impressed you managed to survive this long. It's a nasty world out there now."

He laughed to himself – the gaunt, hollow eyes staring back at him didn't share in his amusement.

"Anyways, you made it this far so each of you are soldiers in my eyes. And you shall be rewarded for your pain – after all, we're basically the British Government.

We can do anything, together. You will all be safe here
– the Infected can't get to you in here. Everyone left in
this room is the last remaining hope for civilization.
Each and every one of you is special, you are the future
of the British people. Right now, my soldiers are out
there, cleaning up the cities so that one day, civilization
can be reborn. But for now, we shall exist in this
building – this will be the basis of our great society."
He paused, looking out to the audience. His eyes rested
on his daughter, Audrey, and a hint of what seemed to
be affection passed over his face for the briefest of
moments.
"But we have ourselves a little problem. What to do
with all of you? Where to house you? Where shall you
sleep?" He looked back out at the crowd.

Some of the children began to scratch at their hands as
if they had suddenly been bitten.

"Allow me to present Hollowgram."
The room darkened. The metal benches folded down
into the ground leaving the crowd lying down on the
floor. No one made a sound.
Everyone was asleep.
Jonathon retreated from the stage and walked back
through the rebuilt BioFlex compound to his offices.

He sat behind his oak desk once more; his new office an exact replica of the one destroyed in the explosion all those months ago.

He opened the journal sat on his desk, entitled Britain 2029. Rummaging in his draw for a pen, he began to write.

'All of this, all of this mess, falls back to 2016. Since that fateful decision to break from Europe, Britain has faced crisis after crisis. In 2017, Britain began its dark descent into populism and then eventually, fascism. People rejected truth and expertise in their masses. Nobody cared about facts, nobody cared about statistics. No, they were just clamouring for change. The broken political system in this once great country has seen the same old, white men in power for generations, never relinquishing their grip on Westminster. And the ordinary people were fed up of this. Weeks of rioting. Unprecedented levels of civil unrest. London gridlocked with protest after protest. And so, in the summer of 2017, the then Prime Minister was ousted in the biggest political shift in history. Change Britain, a populist movement led by the blundering, blustering Charlie McIntosh, stormed to victory, a feat unheard of for a party formed just months before polling day. Change Britain promised some of the most radical reforms to this nation that the country had ever seen. The monarchy was dissolved the next day, their assets seized by the state. The House of Lords – gone too. The government assumed control of all transport, energy and internet companies. Mass deportations of immigrants took place at an unprecedented scale. Change Britain's revolutionary government was being praised to the rafters as levels of unemployment hit the lowest levels in decades. The economy was stronger than it had been in years. People, at last, were *happy.*

It started gradually, but it was there. First, they started censoring any anti – Change Britain media. Social network sites were brought under government control. Every message you sent, every picture you posted, every call you made, filtered by the Government.

And then in 2019 the European War came. Masses of European immigrants flooded through the borders, fleeing violence as Europe slowly burned. It was at this point when fascism really took root at the heart of the British Institution. Religious freedom was outlawed. Freedom of speech was eroded. The official Opposition party banned, and their members arrested. Martial law was declared in every city and public executions became the norm. This was all justified under the 'war effort.'

As the war raged, the economy collapsed, and unemployment shot higher than ever before. Tens of thousands of people lost their homes, bombed out or forced out because they couldn't afford the rent. The population continued to grow at a dangerous level, and disease spread like wildfire.

It was at this point, maybe the winter of 2020 or the spring of 2021, that someone deep within the British Government approached me and asked me to solve the problem of the population.

They told me that they needed to cut the population by a third in order to have any chance of coming back from this crisis.

And so, myself, and the rest of my team at BioFlex, engineered a solution to their problem. We called it Project Vulcan.

Vast camps to imprison people in their thousands, employing tactics used by the British in the Boer, leaving people simply to die as disease and pestilence take root. We started by emptying the prisons into these camps and continuing to arrest anyone that spoke out against the institution. Anyone that didn't fit Change Britain's image was systematically purged from society. Of course, we had to maintain a pretence of normality, so the homeless and the unemployed didn't disappear entirely. But they remained secret for nearly 9 years, until we emptied the last of the camps for Operation Hollowgram. Some had fallen victim to Virus Z-19, others had been liberated by vigilante groups established in the wake of the collapse of society.

That brings me onto the second part of this, Virus Z-19. As the European War raged on through the 2020s, countries began to fall to communism and in some cases, anarchy. The British Government tasked us with designing a biological weapon capable of wiping out an entire continent, permanently.

It had to be incurable, but few diseases were treatable these days anyway since the antibiotics stopped working.

The weapon had entered its final phase of testing when that fateful accident occurred late one night in the BioFlex *compound.*

The virus was never meant to be unleashed on the British people. The government tried to establish a network of safe camps to prevent the spread of disease, separate from Project Vulcan, but these fell within days of the outbreak.
There was no way to save our great nation.'

***

Printed in Great Britain
by Amazon